Yuletide Blend

A Paramour Bay Mystery
Book Ten

KENNEDY LAYNE

YULETIDE BLEND

Copyright © 2019 by Kennedy Layne
Print Edition

DEDICATION

Jeffrey—There's no place like home for the holidays…I love you!

Cole—Always believe in the spirit of Christmas!

Find out who's been naughty or nice in the next snowbound whodunit of the Paramour Bay Mysteries by USA Today Bestselling Author Kennedy Layne...

Stockings are hung by the chimney with care and visions of catnip dance in the air this yuletide season in Paramour Bay. The spirit of giving is in full swing, and the residents of this small coastal Connecticut town are finishing up their last minute holiday shopping.

Raven Marigold takes a break from minding the tea shop to enjoy the winter wonderland the council members have magically created in the middle of town square. The holiday festival has everything from a lighted Christmas tree to singing elves. Even good ol' St. Nick has shown up to hear the wish lists of excited children, but the jolliness in his ho-ho-ho disappears when one of his reindeer goes missing! Is this a reindeer-napping or has the precious animal just wandered off?

Grab a plate of sugar cookies and a glass of milk as Raven and the gang attempt to unwrap the next seasonal whodunit in order to save the cheer for a Merry Christmas this year!

Chapter One

THE FRAGRANT SCENT of fresh-cut pine from the huge selection of Christmas trees hung in the air as eager families searched for just the perfect yuletide tree to celebrate the holiday. The crowded, crushed limestone lot had its perimeter surrounded by long strands of winking colored lights. Streetlamps provided enough illumination on two sides of the corner lot, and a couple of overhead floodlights pointed toward the back over the tree bundling machine to light up the cashier's table.

Selecting the perfect tree from the traditional mom and pop operations was just part of the many fun festivities going on in the busy town square of Paramour Bay. In the summer, the owners ran a small farmers market out of this location that provided many of the townsfolk with fresh produce. Today, they were supplying part of the Christmas joy to all the families awaiting one very special morning.

Most of the fun activities were all tied around certain events, like the snowman building competition or who could make the most original gingerbread house. There was even a small manmade ice rink for those who wanted to skate. Technically, the round area was the small pond in the center of the park that had frozen over. A local vendor had donated the money to build a portable shack to rent skates and sell hot apple cider to patrons.

Several children had constructed bunkers for the ultimate

snowball battles once there had been enough snowfall. It was up to the parks department to keep the combatants contained to willing participants. A well-controlled nightly bonfire was being monitored by the volunteer fire department. Somebody was on watch from six until ten every weekday night, even earlier on weekends. As a matter of fact, a group of Christmas carolers were currently swaying back and forth around the warm blaze as they belted out yet another familiar song.

I hadn't even mentioned the town's twenty-four-foot Christmas tree that already had a lighting ceremony last weekend. Red and gold silk ribbon had been carefully woven between the many branches, and a star that was brighter than an authentic one had been positioned at the very tiptop. Our local electrician, Ned Gardner, made sure all the colored lights, nativity scene, and our star of Bethlehem were in good working order prior to every season. Almost every resident had come to watch the captivating display transform our small-town park into a Norman Rockwell version of a Christmas winter wonderland.

Truthfully, the beautiful blue spruce pine was the fullest I'd ever seen in such a large tree. That was saying a lot, considering that I'd lived in New York City most of my life and the Kennedy Center did the whole holiday tree thing to the limit. Anyway, our town's Christmas tree had even been decorated with the founding families' ornaments from many years past, putting a special touch on the ceremony as something new from each family was added each year.

It was Christmastime in our small, coastal Connecticut town, and the council had gone all out this year. They'd somehow created the perfect winter retreat, and I was loving every minute of it.

Granted, I was a witch. Christian holidays weren't usually

our time to shine, but the winter solstice was just four days prior to Christmas. Of course, I had grown up with the standard Santa stories. I'd learned to appreciate the season for a time of giving and a time of celebration.

My favorite holiday was Halloween, but Christmas fell right behind at a comfortable distance. There was something very magical about this time of year, and I didn't mean that to be a pun of any sort.

I adjusted my scarf a bit to prevent the bitter coastal breeze from hitting my neck directly, mindful of the hot coffee steaming in my left hand. There were no vendor booths selling caffeinated beverages or snacks. There was just hot chocolate for the kids. For those special grownup drinks, the residents needed to head into one of the local stores. This way, the mom and pop shops benefited from any tourists passing through this holiday season. The council members had been wise about only permitting a certain number of electrical access points to maintain a comfortable setting for the children to visit Santa Claus. His area by far was the most magical of all.

A gold and silver glittered path had been created throughout what was supposed to be an enchanting walk through the North Pole. An unused snow-making machine had been stationed next to the mechanical displays of automated polar bears, reindeers, and elves. Mother Nature had provided all the snow we'd ever need this year. The animatronics could be seen moving their heads in adorable ways, some of them actually mimicking the act of loading presents in a large sleigh. Young and old alike got a kick out of the holiday exhibits. The mayor had even been permitted a rescue game park to bring in a small petting zoo with real live reindeer. It had been *the* hit of this year's Christmas winter wonderland thus far, although nothing beat Santa Claus in the starry-eyed boys and girls lining up to tell him what was on their wish list this year.

Bah humbug.

"Just admit it," I said from behind my scarf. "You miss Skippy and his friends this time of year. There's nothing wrong with that, you know. They probably miss you, too."

I'll admit no such thing. They can all go choke on acorns.

While I was attempting to locate the handsome sheriff of our quaint little town, I should probably introduce myself and my cantankerous feline familiar. If he kept up this attitude, I'd have to start calling him the Grinch…or just give him the present I'd bought for him a couple of weeks early. Christmas was still fifteen days away, and Leo's Christmas spirit needed some adjusting.

I won't say no to the gift, if that's what you're worried about. I'm open to bribes.

My familiar's real name is Leo, and I'm Raven Lattice Marigold. This was my second Christmas in Paramour Bay, thanks to my grandmother. I honestly owed her for everything I had right now, from my magical abilities to my small tea shop business on the main thoroughfare of town. There was even the quaint little cottage she'd bequeathed to me in her will. My home sat on the far edge of town, just a stone's throw from the bay.

Why do I suddenly feel like chopped liver? And that is Mr. Leo to the readers, thank you very much.

I held back a laugh as I searched the crowd, grateful that lights had been strung far and wide around the town square park so that it was easy to navigate. You see, Leo had also been bestowed to me, in a manner of speaking. He used to be Nan's familiar, but she'd cast a necromancy spell so that he could stay behind and teach me the ways of our craft. The consequences of dark magic were well known. Unfortunately, Leo had taken the brunt of them as a result.

Even so, Leo handled his idiosyncrasies rather well.

It's not like I had a choice, Raven. Besides, my somewhat gruff appearance earns me special treats from several of the elderly residents in town. I think it's the latest GQ *trend and my resemblance to those men with scruff on their faces in all the stylish fashion magazines. Let's not mess with my good fortune, shall we?*

Leo had been a normal everyday black cat before the necromancy spell. Now? Well, let's just say he resembled something out of one of those *Gremlin* movies from back in the 1980s— after those critters got wet. He had tufts of fur standing out every which away, crooked whiskers, and a tail that resembled a bent coat hanger. He had also somehow managed to acquire orange stripes after having miraculously survived Nan's efforts at casting dark magic. I hadn't even touched on the fact that his left eye bulged out more than his right, and even more so when he was stressed. Combine that with a somewhat selective memory glitch, and he could have been something out of a sci-fi movie assisting Doctor Frankenstein.

All the same, Leo was the best thing that had ever happened to me.

I hate when you do that. It's like putting a fresh coat of paint on an outhouse. You always twist things so that I don't even know which way is up. It's like when the good ol' sheriff tosses me a compliment. I never know what to do with those things. They're like a subscription to Reader's Digest. *They just keep piling up. It's not like I have anything nice to say in return. He's absolutely ordinary in every respect. And don't use this commercial excuse of a holiday to change my mind, either. The spirit of giving? Bah humbug.*

As I'd mentioned earlier, Leo had been in a bad mood for

the last month or so, ever since his nemesis had gone into hibernation. To Leo, that meant he'd lost another annual battle in the squirrelpocalypse to end all wars. That was, until next season.

Go ahead. Rub my failure in my face. That Skippy is a wily opponent. You shouldn't underestimate him. That's how he beats you.

See what I mean?

Well, I had a plan to get Leo out of this funk he was in. I wasn't only bringing Sheriff Liam Drake a cup of coffee in order to steal a kiss, but it was also to distract Leo from his state of melancholy. We were now close enough to the large Christmas tree that my plan should commence in three, two, one...

Lights! All the shiny lights! Thousands of them, Raven, and they twinkle!

All the residents were used to Leo accompanying me everywhere, though he did have the ability to become invisible when he wanted. Seeing as the middle of town square was quite cozy with all the propane-fueled standing heaters positioned in discreet areas, the pads of his paws would be kept safe from the harsh reality of the bitter cold sidewalks and streets. This type of setting was literally a carefree playground for cats, as long as they stayed out of the town's Christmas tree and didn't break any ornaments.

Leo's back end was wiggling in delight as his green, uneven gaze was solely focused on the twinkling lights and shiny trinkets hanging from the branches of the gigantic Christmas tree. It was a good thing the pine was anchored securely so that it couldn't topple over, as well as the ornaments being large enough so that Leo wouldn't be able to knock them to the ground without considerable effort.

"I see Leo is finally in better spirits," Liam said, coming up from behind me to wrap his arms around my waist. My scarf fell below my chin as he rested his cold cheek against mine, though that wasn't surprising since he'd been outside most of the day officially overseeing the town's festivities. "Did you bring me a coffee, Miss Marigold? If yes, then you deserve a kiss."

"Why yes, Sheriff Drake," I replied with a laugh, finally turning around to claim that kiss he'd just promised. "I did make you a special cup of Columbian Supremo."

Liam had already taken the to-go cup from my gloved hand, lifting it to his mouth until he paused in question. He arched an eyebrow before lowering it with just a bit of skepticism.

"Not that kind of special, Liam. You're quite safe from the women's auxiliary."

Those women were quite the teetotalers, every single one of them.

I playfully hit him in the arm, knowing full well that he'd been referring to my holistic tea blends and not alcohol. My Nan had gotten into the business when she'd wanted to use her craft to help the residents of Paramour Bay, and I'd naturally followed in her footsteps. Well, maybe with a few bumps along the way. Witchcraft wasn't necessarily easy for an accident-prone witch.

Anyway, those townsfolk who suffered from arthritis now had a few extra skips in their steps, just as those with common colds found they could drink a certain tea and feel better within a fairly short time period. There was nothing more rewarding than to know my gift could help others, and that included most of the members of the women's auxiliary.

I guess you could say I was their own personal Mrs. Claus, bestowing the gift of health whenever I could.

I'd been given a gift, as well—Liam's acceptance of who and

what I was. It was a relief to no longer need to hide my lineage from someone who was important to me.

"How was your day?" Liam asked, enjoying the rich Columbian coffee I'd made him right before closing up the shop. "Did you have a steady stream of traffic?"

"Yes, and sales were fantastic," I replied, very pleased with the holiday sale I'd been running on my seasonal inventory. "Otis even came into the shop today to special order a few accessories that Karen has been wanting to add to her tea collection. Hey, did your sister get back to you about spending the holidays here?"

Otis and Karen Finley had raised Liam and his sister after they'd lost their mother in the middle of their teenage years. Liam had even followed in Otis' footsteps, entering the New York City Police Academy. Upon Otis' retirement as sheriff of Paramour Bay, Liam had returned home to take his position as the town's only peace officer.

"My sister has decided that she's taking that trip to Europe that she's been putting off for years. Said something about the ticket prices being too good to pass up." Liam lifted a hand when Monty, who owned the hardware store across the street, called out hello to us. "Are we still on for dinner at the diner? Trixie has shepherd's pie on the menu for this weekend only as a special holiday treat."

You distracted me on purpose, Raven. That wasn't very nice.

"Six-thirty sound good?" I asked, wondering why Leo was back so quick. He'd plopped himself down next to me, licking his paw and eyeing me with disgust. I glanced over my shoulder to make sure that the Christmas tree was still intact and not on fire. I was pretty certain that he couldn't do any harm to it, but one could never be sure. I breathed a sigh of relief when every ornament still seemed to be in one piece. "I have some errands I want to—"

"What could be wrong now?" Liam muttered underneath his breath when there seemed to be a bit of commotion over by the petting zoo. "First, one of the ice sculptures was knocked over, and now this. Little Bobby Hurst better not have fed those reindeer any more candy canes. He already tried to give them a dose of sugar from the sugar cookies, much to the dismay of the owner."

I winced when I realized I hadn't thought this whole distraction thing through with Leo. What if Bobby Hurst hadn't been the reason everyone seemed to be scattering in every random direction? Had Leo somehow managed to convince the reindeer into stampeding through town?

I'd gladly take credit where credit is due, but I didn't have a thing to do with whatever is going on over there. Honestly, I'm offended you would even think such a thing. Reindeer? I'm too busy trying to come up with a new plan for the spring offensive to stop the impending squirrelpocalypse.

"Really?" I asked Leo, not worrying about other people seeing me talk to my cat since their sole focus was on all the hullabaloo on the opposite side of town square. Liam had already begun making his way through the throngs of residents now vying for a good place to see what all the uproar was about. "You chased Mindy's tabby rescue all through her boutique until Cupcake had clawed her way through most of the sweater rack."

That orange hairball looked at me wrong. What was I supposed to do? You can't let that kind of thing slide. It just mushrooms from there if you don't put your paw down!

"Cupcake is only a year and a half old and twice as small as you," I countered, hoping that Leo would see that his actions bordered on violent intimidation. I understood that he was simply looking for a distraction to occupy his time now that his yearly battle with the local squirrels had been postponed until the spring, but that didn't give him the right to terrorize the quite ordinary domestic pets around town. "What we need is a good mystery to keep you occupied."

Have you lost your ever-loving mind? Never mind. I already know the answer to that question. It was a casualty of your first day in town.

"I'm not jinxing us," I replied confidently, already knowing that Leo was referring to karma. I wasn't worried in the least about tempting our fate, though. Once Halloween had come and gone, Paramour Bay had been peacefully quiet and devoid of any murders, thefts, or arsons related to the supernatural. "I was thinking more along the lines of a small mystery. You know, maybe helping Elsie find her favorite pair of reading glasses. They've been missing for the last two days. Besides, there are other mysteries to solve besides the odd murder."

The Halloween debacle was a long story, but I could summarize. You see, my great aunt still belonged to the Windsor coven, the members of which just so happened to be at war with one another. I'd officially gotten Aunt Rowena to believe that me, my mother, and my friends wanted no part in a war between the two factions. I'd finally grown a backbone and managed to use it properly.

Uh, Raven?

I looked down at Leo, waiting for a snarky comment about my confidence level having inched up a bit over the last month and a half. Instead, his left eye protruded a bit as he stared at something behind me.

Don't do it. Don't turn around. And if you do, which I know you will, I'd like to go on record that it wasn't me. I had nothing to do with chasing that mouse up his pant leg.

With that kind of introduction, I couldn't help myself. I looked over my shoulder to find Santa Claus himself standing behind me looking a bit melancholy as worry lines appeared between his bushy eyebrows. I have to say I was pretty impressed with the likeness from the pictures. The council had done a fantastic job of picking this particular Santa out of the cast of characters we usually had.

If you say so. Personally, I think his beard could have been a bit longer.

"I should apologize on Leo's behalf," I began, pausing long enough to search for the right words. What could one say when their cat wreaked havoc on a holiday display? "He's been a bit lonely ever since the local squirrels went into hibernation, and he's just looking for something to keep him busy."

"No need to apologize, dear," Santa Claus replied with a smile that didn't quite reach his blue eyes. We stood in silence for a moment, observing the crowd as they all began to fan out in groups around town square. Something had definitely happened at the petting zoo, and Liam was directing the horde. "My lead reindeer has gone missing."

You might want to step away slowly, Raven. Make no sudden moves toward him. It appears that this Santa Claus is taking his duties a little bit too seriously, if you get my drift. The opioid problem is striking everywhere and affecting people on all walks of life.

"Missing?" I was pretty sure that this Santa Claus hadn't been close enough to the petting zoo to know what exactly had happened to cause all the commotion. A thought occurred to me. "Is this one of the activities scheduled for tonight? Find the red-nosed reindeer? That's a clever one."

"I would never use my reindeer in such a manner, my dear." Santa had topped his outfit off with those gold-rimmed glasses, which he now adjusted on the end of his bulbous nose. "The sheriff believes that my lead reindeer has just wandered off, but I don't believe that to be the case. This doesn't bode well for my trip around the world. How will I find my way through the fog and snow?"

Are we really going to stand here and listen to this malarkey? Raven, it's obvious he's a few presents shy of a full sleigh. We don't even know that one of those antlered brutes is missing.

"Raven, could you go look in the alleyway behind the shops?" Liam called out, pointing toward *Tea, Leaves, & Eves.* There was a narrow alleyway that ran behind my tea shop for regular deliveries to most of the stores. "One of the reindeer has gone missing."

Coincidence. Merely coincidence, Raven. He could have guessed.

"How did you…" My voice trailed off as I realized Santa Claus was no longer in my vicinity. A quick look revealed that he was making his way back to his throne where some of the children were lining back up to pay him a personal visit now that their parents were distracted. It appeared that duty called, but I'd love to know how he knew about the reindeer. "Odd."

It's not surprising. You do tend to attract the more eccentric sort.

It didn't take me long to check the alleyway. A few other residents had done the same, and we made our way back to town square in a small group. I managed to spot Liam still standing near the petting zoo, so I made my way over to him to let him know that I was willing to do whatever I could to help facilitate the safe return of the reindeer.

"What happened?" I asked after letting him know that there

was no sign of the large animal in the alleyway. "Did someone unlatch the gate?"

"The owner isn't sure," Liam replied, unhooking the flashlight from his utility belt. He handed it to me, already ensuring that the switch had been turned on. "He did a head count, which he claims to do every fifteen minutes. One of the reindeer is missing, but the gate wasn't open. I'm fairly sure that he didn't fly out of the pen, either. Everyone in the vicinity is claiming they didn't see a thing. The mayor is with the owner now, reassuring him that we'll have this situation resolved in a matter of a few minutes."

I glanced back over to where Santa was listening intently to a little girl's list of Christmas wishes, deciding not to burden Liam with my suspicions. My palm hadn't reacted in any way, so the Santa Claus whom the town council had hired bore no ill intentions toward the residents or the animals. I might have forgotten to mention that energy formed in the palm of my right hand whenever danger was near, and no such reaction was happening at the moment.

If you recall, we have determined that your witch-signal is a bit defective at times.

"Leo and I will go check the alleyway behind the tea shop again," I promised, lacking any better alternative. I adjusted my scarf for the upcoming search. "I mean, how hard can it be to find a reindeer in Paramour Bay?"

You realize that this might be the consequences of that jinx you wrangled up earlier.

"Leo, I didn't jinx us," I disputed as we came upon the sidewalk, stepping up while being mindful of any slick spots. "One of the children could have simply opened the gate to the pen when the owner wasn't looking. Like you said, the reindeer probably walked away in hopes of finding Bobby Hurst and another dose of sugar. I imagine that caribous are very highly intelligent animals."

You must be thinking about Skippy and his tribe of ninja squirrels, because you couldn't possibly be referring to those thick antlered brutes. Have you seen the size of those things? Their noses are bigger than my face, which doesn't leave a lot of room for brains. I bet they can sniff out a granular speck of sugar from a mile away. We should check the bakery.

It was a good thing I could hide my smile behind my scarf, because I'm pretty sure that Leo was attempting to figure out which direction the reindeer had wandered off. My plan of distracting him had worked, just a little differently than I had originally planned. Truthfully, the bakery wasn't such a bad idea. I did have to wonder how no one had seen a five-hundred-pound animal walking out of our rather crowded town square.

This is where the jinx comes in, Raven. Don't you see? You might have actually gotten us involved with an honest-to-goodness reindeer-napping!

Chapter Two

"I HEARD ABOUT all the commotion last night. Did they ever find poor Rudy?" Heidi Connolly asked as she breezed into the tea shop the next morning. She was wearing one of her expensive pantsuits from when she'd lived in New York City. Either she had an appointment with one of the founding families of our little town or she was making a day trip into the Big Apple for business. "Hi, Leo. Did you know that Cupcake now has her own pink, fluffy pillow in the boutique's display window? I don't know why you don't like her. She's got the sweetest disposition, always eager to be scratched behind her ears."

My best friend was a like a mini-tornado of glitter and all things frivolous—invariably full of energy and optimism. She was one of the only two humans who I'd informed of my not-so-recently discovered supernatural secret. Not that I was part of my ancestors' coven, but confiding in Heidi and Liam had gone against one of the top five rules established by the governing council, which was a fairly common stance taken by most organized covens from what I understood. Needless to say, I wasn't my fellow witches' and warlocks' most favorite person, not that they were fully aware of my indiscretions.

That orange con artist has everyone fooled, even my beloved Heidi. This moment of realization has brought a tear to my slightly bulging eye. I'm not sure how, but this has all got to be tied in with the squirrelpocalypse. I'm going to be forced to invade my emergency edible catnip treat supply, aren't I? I was saving those for a truly momentous occasion. They are the last of my one-time organic Honduran premium acquisition. Truly a primo year for the Honduran crop, you know. Unequalled in decades of experimental catnip quality enhancement efforts.

"Get this," Heidi said before I could answer her, walking straight to the small coffee station I'd set up in order for my customers to sample a variety of products. "I have a meeting with Cora Barnes to go over her year-end numbers. I thought for sure she was going to find another accountant when she discovered that I was the one who'd taken over the firm from Beetle. It's not like I haven't tried to touch base with everyone in town, but Cora never saw fit to respond to any of my calls. Yesterday afternoon? Bam! There was this voice message out of nowhere, asking for a meeting."

Okay, the reason for the coffee samples might have been a tiny white lie. I'd always been a covert coffee lover through and through. Besides, I'd made sure that the coffee selection only took up one of the high-top tables so that could I maintain the original tenor of my Nan's tea shop. I was currently expanding our selection of premium coffee station accruements, while ensuring that we continued to provide for the experienced tea aficionado.

"Cora only has a problem with my mother, as far as I know," I refuted from my position on the stool behind the counter. I then thought over my statement. "Well, she doesn't like me very much either, but you've got the experience of a major New York City firm backing you up. That's prestigious in the eyes of her circle. Cora and Desmond Barnes would never forego that kind of opportunity to up their ante.'"

Heidi had cut a deal with her old firm, and the contract she'd put in place had definitely been a goldmine. She had the best of both worlds while owning her own business, taking over an established setup that Beetle had structured here in our small town, all the while living close to her best friend. I wasn't sure what had been included in the fine print of the sale of the town's only bookkeeping business, but it had definitely been to her advantage from the looks of Heidi's new briefcase.

"I never thought of it that way," Heidi said with a frown, probably pondering if maybe Cora didn't think she was up to the task of handling the malt shop's accounting needs. "I better be ready with my A game. A good word from her could bring in new business from some of those lakefront property owners."

Heidi finished adding a few sugar cubes and a dollop of fresh cream from a small ceramic pitcher that I kept out on my new Peltier chill plate I'd plugged in over on the high-top table. She then made sure to grab a hardwood stir stick before joining me at the counter. She'd gotten her hair cut recently by Candy, our local hairstylist, and it was shaped in the cutest bob that had an abundance of loose curls framing her face.

"How's Jack been?" I asked, setting down my pen on top of the town map I'd collected from the back. Usually, I used the various maps stored in the inventory room to locate missing items. Unfortunately, I didn't have anything from the reindeer that I could utilize in order to scry for his location. No one had been able to find him, and Liam had been forced to call the sheriffs in the surrounding towns to be on the lookout for a five-hundred-pound Norwegian reindeer with a sweet tooth. "Did you finally meet his parents for dinner?"

You just had to bring up that oaf of a detective. Is there a reason that you don't want me to have a good morning? Any chance you want to wrap my paws in tape to amuse the local cretins?

"No," Heidi frowned, carefully setting her briefcase on the floor while managing not to spill a drop of her coffee. I usually wasn't so graceful. "Jack got called out to an armed robbery case that turned into a prolonged hostage situation. We had to reschedule. I'm telling you, it's fate. Mrs. F doesn't want me to meet his parents."

It's nice to see that my karma is turning around for the better. Hey, where is my BFF? He's due to come into work this morning, right?

"Fate has nothing to do with two canceled dinners," I reassured Heidi, reaching for my own cup of coffee. "It has everything to do with Jack's crazy schedule that is inherent with his kind of work. Leo, Beetle should be here any moment with your morning treats."

Heidi was used to me carrying on two different conversations at once. It hadn't always been so easy in the beginning, but now it had come to be second nature.

As for Leo's BFF and my part-time employee, that would be Beetle. Think the mad scientist from *Back to the Future*, white hair and all. The only difference was that Beetle had an affinity for bowties, cardigan sweaters, and a tendency to repeat words when talking. He was also the one who owned the accounting firm before selling it to Heidi. The only reason he worked a few days a week for me was to keep busy, but I wasn't sure how long he'd be under my employment now that my mother was back in the picture. After all, he was courting her.

That's right—Beetle was now engaged to my mother. The very woman who once said a team of wild horses couldn't drag her back to this town.

You hate me, don't you? Next, you'll bring up that pixie leaving her sprinkles of glitter on my fur!

I tried unsuccessfully not to laugh, commiserating with Leo fully on his list of taboo subjects. With that said, Leo thought of Beetle as his own personal supplier of addictive feline edible treats, all of which were liberally laced with catnip. My familiar wasn't going to be worrying about anything after he'd consumed his special morning delicacy. It was sweet, really. Beetle always brought Leo a catnip edible to start his day.

My BFF gets me. We have that kind of bond, like all kindred spirits do.

"What's that?" Heidi asked, nodding toward the map in front of me. She looked over her shoulder as if to see who else was around when she knew darn well that I'd just flipped over the open sign. She then feigned we were conspiring against the world when she lifted a hand to hide her lips. "Who are we looking for now?"

"Rudy, if you get my drift," I replied, touching my nose. "The reindeer that escaped his pen last night is still on the lam. Liam had all the residents searching into the wee hours. The owner, whose name is Barry Mina, was just beside himself. I guess his family is Norwegian, or maybe one of those other Scandinavian countries. I'm not sure."

"How far could a large animal like that get?" Heidi asked with a confused frown, looking at the map upside down. She pointed to one of our least favorite places. "I mean, reindeer can't fly, can they? Did anyone check the cemetery? That place is usually deserted—from living people, that is."

I'll ask Ivan. Our weekly poker game is tonight, though the resident warlock won't be in attendance. He's on some odd mission for the Wicked Witch of Windsor. And before you ask, no—I didn't question him about the family related subjects we've been hoping to ignore.

"What did Leo say?" Heidi asked, taking a sip of her coffee.

"His weekly poker game with the ghouls is tonight," I relayed with a smile, wishing Leo hadn't told me about Rye Marigold and his work with the coven's warring factions. He was the warlock who wouldn't be playing in tonight's game. "Rye is apparently out of town, running errands for my Aunt Rowena."

"You're the one who insisted you didn't want any part of that war," Heidi pointed out, though I knew her to be in full agreement. "Let them do whatever it is they're going to do. Besides, your mother is keeping an eye on the situation. She can handle your aunt."

My mother, whom I had a love/hate relationship with, had moved to Paramour Bay last month after becoming engaged to Beetle. She had previously agreed wholeheartedly that we shouldn't and wouldn't get involved in coven business, but she was never one to be kept in a box. She preferred to know what was going on around her at all times, with freedom of action ultimately her chief concern, even though she was the one who'd left town at the young age of twenty-three. She'd sworn she was giving up witchcraft, raising me without any knowledge of the supernatural, until it had all blown up in her face when Nan made me beneficiary of her estate and the family legacy.

Now the Mistress of the Dark has returned to lure my BFF over to the dark side. We need to save him, Raven. Would you at all be interested in poisoning your mother? I mean, we have the perfect beverage at our disposal. I'm sure it wouldn't be hard to put a few drops of poison into a cup of tea.

"Beetle has no idea about the Marigold lineage," I reminded Leo, hoping that it stayed that way. Beetle reminded me of a nervous nelly, so there was no telling what he'd do if he discovered the existence of the supernatural. "Can we just focus on the missing reindeer for now? Heidi, the answer to your question about searching the cemetery is a yes. Liam had groups assigned to each and every area around town. There was no sign of Randy."

"Randy?" Heidi asked, confusion written all over her face. "I thought we were looking for Rudy. Are there two missing reindeer?"

I'm still looking for my BFF, but he's nowhere to be found, either. And here I sit, withering away into nothingness.

Santa Claus had definitely gotten into my head last night. I kept coming back to that peculiar conversation, thinking that maybe the man was part owner of the petting zoo or something like that. I'd have to ask Liam to check for me.

"The reindeer that's missing is actually named Randy." I set my coffee cup back down on the counter when I saw Pearl walking out of the diner. "I was just referencing the famous red-nosed type reindeer. 'Tis the season and all that jazz."

Bah humbug. Where is my BFF?

I hopped down from my stool and then adjusted the thick green belt that I'd put on my waist to accessorize my turtleneck. I'd found it in the sale bin at the boutique, and I hadn't been able to pass it up.

"Give me a second," I quipped to Piper, walking toward the strings of ivory-colored fairies that prevented my customers from seeing into the back room. Nan had enchanted them with magic, a glyph of warding to be specific, thus protecting the area where she used to create her holistic blends. "Pearl is walking this way. Her eye doctor gave her progressive lenses, and she's not happy about it."

"Are you telling me that you can restore wayward eyesight with one of your spells?"

You might want to warn her that there is a chance that Purple Pearl could end up cross-eyed. No offense, Raven.

"My track record for spells is finally going in a positive direction, Leo, and you know it," I called out over my shoulder. In full confession, I might have gotten off to a rocky start in my witchcraft lessons. "Heidi, I'm not to the point where I can miraculously heal the blind. On the plus side, I'm getting really good at the progression of health. Take Otis and his arthritis. He took up ice fishing again this month, after not doing it for close to ten years."

While carrying on the conversation, I'd reached through the ivory-colored fairy beads for Pearl's package that I'd set on the edge of the table. I was pretty pleased with the holiday presentation, including the sparkling red bows I'd gotten for a good price at the hobby store.

"This time next year, Pearl will be back in her bifocals," I replied confidently, setting Pearl's package next to the cash register. I flashed a smile. "I love my job."

"Hello, dear hearts," Pearl exclaimed, sailing through the entrance of the tea shop as if she owned the place. "Look at my most recent find from my trip into New Haven. It's the perfect shade of silver to match my lovely hair."

Come to think of it, Raven, you should have added something in that spell that rectified Purple Pearl's colorblindness. Scratch that. Can you imagine waking up and looking into the mirror to find that you went from silver to purple hair? Heart attack city.

Leo did have a point, but I would never add something to a holistic blend without the approval of the customer. Pearl had chosen a shade of what she'd thought was silver, only for it to turn out purple. Nothing Candy had said could change Pearl's mind. Needless to say, Pearl now walked around town in all her glory with purple hair that she truly believed was silver.

"I love it, Pearl," Heidi exclaimed, having learned early on to go with the flow. "The fabric shimmers like a blanket of freshly fallen snow. Spectacular! Hey, where's Harold this morning?"

"Harold got dressed in his winter gear and headed out first thing this morning with Eugene and Alfred." Pearl adjusted the lapel on her dress coat so that her scarf rested against the material just right, pleased with Heidi's compliment. "They're out looking for that poor reindeer that went missing. They've convinced themselves over too many drinks last night that they are the only ones who can find him. My bet is that they won't last past lunchtime. You know how Albert needs his nap."

I'm just throwing this out there, but couldn't the good ol' sheriff just follow the trail of brownie piles? We domesticated felines know how to cover up our tracks, but antlered brutes such as good ol' Randy? Not so much.

It was times like these that Leo astounded me with his cleverness.

It's the premium organic catnip, not that I've had my treats this morning. You don't think that antlered brute has anything to do with why my BFF is running late, do you?

"You'd think there would be some sign left of such a large animal," I reiterated, concurring that there should have been something dropped somewhere in town. I even made a circle with both hands to indicate a round pile. "You know..."

Heidi and Pearl both pulled their faces in disgust, but then shared a look that indicated they agreed with that assessment.

"On that note and while I'm all for adventure, there is no way that I'm sinking my Michael Kors boots into a pile of reindeer sludge." Heidi leaned down and retrieved her briefcase, keeping her to-go cup securely in her hand. She should put the leather gloves on that she'd gotten on sale at the boutique, but she only had to walk next door for her meeting with Cora. "Wish me luck. If Rudy is still missing after my appointment, I'll drive home to change clothes and help with the search party. Is Beetle coming in today?"

"It's Randy, and yes," I replied, accepting the twenty-dollar bill that Pearl had retrieved from her wallet. It didn't take me long to ring up her purchase. "Text me, and I'll let you know where I am."

Heidi lifted her coffee cup in goodbye, using her shoulder to push open the glass door.

"How is your mother settling in?" Pearl asked, taking the change I'd handed her. She quickly and efficiently slid the single dollars inside her wallet and the change into the pouch. "She was a wild one in her youth, that one."

Please tell Purple Pearl not to bring up such unpleasant memories. At least, not on an empty stomach.

Leo and I both had breakfast this morning before leaving the cottage. Don't think for one moment that I'd let him starve.

I don't recall there being dinner on the table at precisely seven o'clock last Friday. By seven twenty-one, I could barely move. You have no sense of time, nor of my needs, for that matter.

Don't let Leo sucker you into believing that I neglected him in any way. I'd only been thirty minutes late getting home from a nice dinner with Liam.

Thirty-three minutes. I had just enough strength left to look at the clock.

"You'll have to tell me all about her misspent youth one of these days," I said with a smile, wondering what kind of ammunition there was in those sordid tales. I needed all the help I could get when it came to staying one step ahead of my mother. No matter how much I believed she wanted to help stave off any remnants of a coven war from spilling into Paramour Bay, she usually had an ulterior motive. "Here you go. I do believe this tea blend will help your eyesight as well, Pearl."

"I can't stand these progressive lenses. They give me a headache," Pearl complained, pushing up the purple-rimmed frames that were perched delicately on the bridge of her nose. "I'll be sure to have a hot cup of tea every night. You truly believe this holistic blend will help improve my eyesight?"

"Without a doubt," I assured her, finally catching sight of Beetle walking by the display window.

Sweet angel of mercy, it's about time.

Leo had practically been face-planted in his bed, but he scurried back on his two front paws until he was sitting at attention with his left eye focused solely on the entrance of the shop. I wasn't one to talk about addiction when I couldn't get through a single morning without my mug of fresh coffee.

"You have a good day, dear," Pearl said after having put on her lavender-colored gloves that she assumed were a light greyish silver. She then picked up her holistic tea blend that I'd put in the cutest brown bag with the *Tea, Leaves, & Eves* insignia branded on the front, with a sparkling red bow that added a nice seasonal touch. "Stay warm if you intend to go searching for that sweet caribou. Dreadful that he's gone missing this time of year."

Beetle had seen that Pearl was heading his way, so he opened the door for her and waited until she'd crossed the threshold before seeking warmth. He bent slightly, as if bowing, and then wished her a good morning before allowing the door to close.

I'm pretty sure my tufts of fur were turning grey. Could my BFF move any slower? Raven, we'll need to work on a tea blend that gives my supplier an oomph to his step. Come to think it, something of that nature could work in our favor. He might have enough vigor to kick your mother right in the—

"Good morning, my dear Raven," Beetle exclaimed cheerfully, unravelling his scarf. "Good morning. I just had the most peculiar run-in with Santa Claus."

Raven, don't you dare distract my BFF from his most important task of the day and his duly-appointed rounds.

"Santa Claus?" I asked, doing my best to give Beetle time to remove his dress coat. He'd already walked over to the display window, where Leo was eyeing me with daggers. Knowing the only way that Leo was going to be of any help to me today was if he had a moment to enjoy his favorite edible on the planet, I managed to bite my lip until I heard Leo sigh with contentment. "You mean, the man who was dressed as Santa Claus for last night's festivities?"

"The one and only," Beetle said with a beaming smile, giving Leo a pat on the head before leaving him to enjoy his treat. "The odd thing about our short conversation was the message he wanted me to relay to you. Yes, very odd indeed."

I waited for the palm of my right hand to become warm or develop those piercing tingles that always caused my skin to itch, but it remained cool to the touch. I'd chalked up my conversation with Santa last night as a mere happenstance, but I was now beginning to think there was more to the man than met the eye.

"What was the message, Beetle?"

I'm ready for anything after that special treat. My BFF sure knows the good stuff from the generic. He deserves a holiday bonus, Raven.

"Well, Santa Claus wanted you to know that his trip around

the world to deliver joy to all the little boys and girls depends on finding his lead reindeer," Beetle paraphrased, looking a bit befuddled by the cryptic message. He began to remove his jacket as he walked toward the back room, the white ends of his hair floating to and from on top of his head. "I'm not sure why he wanted you to know that, my dear Raven. He then mentioned joining the search would be the distraction you're looking for, which I found strangely peculiar. Very peculiar indeed. Do you happen to know him personally?"

My surprised gaze focused instantly on Leo, who was staring at me in horror with bits of loose catnip stuck to the ends of his whiskers. I'm almost positive that I didn't say aloud my wish for Leo to have a distraction from his pining after Skippy and his minions. Did I?

I should have known, Raven. I should have known all along that Skippy and his ninja squirrels wouldn't let a winter hibernation keep them from their diabolical plan to rule the world. Don't you see? Santa Claus is doing Skippy's bidding, luring me into a false sense of security in the off-season. Santa Claus has gone over to the dark side, and we shall now call him Santa Vader!

Chapter Three

"GOOD MORNING, EILEEN." I greeted the town's dispatcher with a smile. I wasn't surprised to see that she was wearing one of her holiday-themed sweaters. This one looked different somehow. An embroidered Christmas tree actually had strings of lights that twinkled sewn into the branches. It was quite mesmerizing for all of three seconds, but then it caused my eyes to hurt. "Love the sweater. Did you add something new?"

Do you have to encourage her? Those lights can cause an epileptic seizure in certain familiars who are predisposed to that condition. I shouldn't have to tell you these things.

"Thank you, Raven," Eileen said over the ringing phone, beaming with happiness that I'd noticed she'd made changes to her apparel. "I changed out the bulbs so that the colors were brighter, along with a white light for the star. Doesn't it look so much better?"

Debatable.

"It certainly stands out," I concurred, stepping through the half swinging door that had been part of the original structure. "Any news on Randy?"

"Not even a single sighting." Eileen shook her head in sadness as the office phone rang once more. "I've been helping Liam coordinate the search parties, sending them to the tips we've been getting from all the neighborhoods. Nothing has turned up yet, though."

There's a reason for that, Raven. This is all a massive conspiracy.

"Beetle is covering the tea shop today so that I can help out. Let me say hi to Liam and then I'm all yours."

Good. We can utilize the good ol' sheriff's resources to find out the real name behind that red suit. Once we have that, we can expose him for who he really is—a mere pawn in the squirrelpocalypse.

Eileen acknowledged that she'd heard me, but she was already answering the next call. I walked toward Liam's office, which was always open. I wondered briefly if the door had ever been closed. He wasn't formal, and even the residents called him by his first name instead of the official title on his door.

"...already touched base with Animal Control." Liam was standing behind his desk and talking on his phone while bent over a map. "I'll keep you updated throughout the day if anything turns up."

I quietly crossed the hardwood floor, taking my gloves off while he finished up his conversation. The only individuals who would want to be kept up-to-date throughout the day was either the mayor or Barry, the owner of the Norwegian reindeer.

"Yes, sir. I'll do that." Liam stole a kiss when I came around the desk as he continued to listen to the other half of the conversation. His gaze caught sight of Leo as he materialized in one of the guest chairs. "I think tonight at seven o'clock, but I'll double check with Eileen. I'll have her call you to confirm."

I vaguely remember a local television station being scheduled to come into town to do a segment on Paramour Bay's winter wonderland. It was no wonder the mayor was so concerned about a missing caribou. A special interest story of that nature would overshadow the entire event.

I wonder if I can get the news anchor to do a segment on the squirrelpocalypse. Skippy has control over most of the major media outlets, but a small independent news crew might be willing to take a chance.

"Good morning, you two," Liam greeted after replacing the receiver back on its stand. "I was just about to head over to the tea shop. Is there, um, anything you can do to locate this missing reindeer?"

Liam used his quote fingers to emphasize the word "do" in his last statement. He was referring to using witchcraft, but there wasn't a thing we could do without having something on hand that belonged to Randy.

I bet we can find a pile of his special homemade brownies in the pen.

Randy wasn't the only reindeer that had been kept in the relatively large enclosure in town square. There was no way that I was going to try and figure out which pile of excrement belonged to which caribou.

I never thought I'd say this, but now would be a perfect time to call on your mother. Isn't she always saying that she wants to help us solve these mysteries? Well, there's no time like the present. Not that I'm going to be distracted from my main purpose here, mind you. I know Skippy and his crew are involved in this somehow.

"I can only do a location spell if I have something of Randy's, which is why I'm hoping that you'll give me the contact information of Barry Mina," I said, knowing that it went against Liam's code of ethics to give out personal data on an individual involved in an official ongoing case. "Barry is the owner of the petting zoo, so he might be able to supply a blanket or specific food bowl of some sort that I can use to scry."

I'll admit, the thought of having my mother sort through

mountains of reindeer punky was tempting.

Say no more! I'm on it.

Leo disappeared as quickly as he'd materialized, leaving Liam and I to stare after him in horror for completely different reasons. Liam was still getting used to this whole witchcraft thing, but I was stunned at how eager Leo was to get one up on my mother. I shouldn't be, given their history of antagonizing one another.

"Don't ask," I muttered, looking up at Liam with hope. "Oh, there's one more thing I was hoping you'd be able to get me."

"Absolutely not," Liam said firmly, emphatically shaking his head. "You are not getting another hint about your Christmas present. My lips are sealed."

I rested my hand over my scarf, comforted by the fact that the necklace Liam had given me on my birthday was securely clasped around my neck. He'd known that I'd been wanting a black tourmaline, but that I'd been searching for just the right one. Well, he'd not only found the perfect crystal, but the black stone he'd acquired dated back to the middle 1600s. It had actually belonged to Sarah Good, the very one who'd been involved in the infamous Salem witch coven.

To stress just how important this particular crystal was to my safety, Nan had managed to pierce the veil to get a message to me from the other side during All Hallows' Eve. That specific holiday was when the veil between us and the afterlife was at its thinnest. These planes of existence, the places from which witches draw their power, are called inner planes. They are connected to our existence by the ethereal plane.

There are many names for the outer planes that humans understood to be heaven and hell. Nan was at rest on an outer plane that we understood to be reached through established conduits; however, there are other magical ways to travel through the astral plane to reach her. Of course, Nan's message had been oddly vague due to the distortion of time and distance. I still didn't know exactly what she meant…other than I wasn't ever to take this necklace off.

"Hey, I didn't mean to worry you," Liam said softly, knowing all about what happened this past All Hallows' Eve.

"You didn't," I said with a smile, putting aside my worry to focus on the safety of the missing reindeer. "And as much as I want another hint on my Christmas gift, the favor I need actually has to do with Santa Claus."

"Santa Claus? You mean, the ol' jolly man himself?"

"I was hoping you could tell me what his real name is, along with an address or maybe a number."

I'm back, and I just have to say that giving your mother a pair of elbow length gloves was the highlight of my day thus far.

Liam startled at Leo's sudden appearance. I could commiserate, because it had taken me quite a long time to get used to those in and out blips myself.

"Leo, I'll deal with you later," I warned, putting a call to my mother at the top of my list of to-do things for the day. I didn't believe for a second that she would fall for some story that would have her sifting through mounds of doodoo. "Well, what do you say? Do you think you can get me his name and address?"

Come to think of it, the Mistress of the Dark did seem a little too enthusiastic about sifting through those piles of steaming brownies.

"The mayor's assistant would have the information on everyone involved in the town square festivities," Liam explained, deflating my hope just a bit. "Sheila was the one to do the hiring, but I can try to get you whatever information you might need. I can't promise you anything, though. Am I missing something? What does St. Nick have to do with the lost reindeer?"

"Probably nothing, but I had a somewhat disconcerting conversation with him last night. I know this sounds silly, but this Santa Claus made it sound as if he truly believed he was the genuine article." I shrugged when Liam ran a hand down his face in disbelief. In his defense, his life had been turned upside down recently with the whole supernatural secret thing being exposed. "Plus, Beetle ran into him this morning. Somehow, Santa knew that Beetle worked for me and wanted him to relay a message about this mystery being the distraction I'd been hoping for. I need to find out who he is."

You're making Santa Claus sound like a psycho, which probably isn't far off the mark.

"Raven, you do understand that this man sounds—"

"Santa isn't a stalker or a psycho, so there's no need to call the men in the white jackets," I reassured Liam, realizing that everything I'd just said pointed to a deranged man wearing a red suit. "Kris Kringle did a fantastic job with the children last night. I was just hoping that he had something to do with the petting zoo. You know, maybe part owner or something. He was really concerned that…well, that his lead reindeer had gone missing."

Look, there's nothing wrong with a slightly senile Santa. Maybe I can even convince him that he should leave a few extra packets of premium organic catnip under the tree. Granted, it's never a good idea to invite someone to come down the chimney who might actually decide to take us up on that offer, but we do have a volunteer fire department for those types of things.

It was a good thing that Liam couldn't hear Leo or else I wouldn't be getting any information pertaining to Santa Claus. It took a few more minutes of finagling, along with a promise to only speak to the jolly man later during tonight's festivities, but Liam finally promised he'd get me a name. There was no mention of an address or number, but I understood the reason he was so reluctant to do so.

"I'm going to go home and change," I told him, lifting myself up on the tips of my toes to steal another kiss. "Wearing a skirt in this weather isn't such a good idea, and I also want to change into a warmer pair of boots. Heidi bought me a pair of Ugg boots for Christmas last year. No time like the present to wear them."

"Eileen gave out hand warmers this morning to the volunteer searchers. Make sure you grab some." Liam settled his dark gaze on Leo. "Your job is to keep her safe out there."

It's like he doesn't even know you...

"See you later," I called out, not bothering to relay Leo's message. I could admit to there being a couple of times when I'd gotten us into a pickle, but we always managed to come out the other end in one piece. "I'll keep in touch."

You mean, we're the end of the pickle that doesn't get eaten? The part with the stem on it? That's what you consider in one piece? Wow. Just wow, Raven.

"Eileen, I was thinking about creating another group." A quick glance over my shoulder as I left Liam's office told me that Leo had made himself invisible. "I'm going home to change clothes, but I can convince Ted and my mother to join me. Heidi's meeting with Cora should be over within the hour, so she can tag along, too."

I haven't mentioned Ted, have I? Where do I even begin?

At the far-left side of your average Crayola box?

I wouldn't describe Ted in those words. He was a gentle giant with a heart of gold, who just so happened to be a wax golem.

I was there when that candlestick was made. Trust me, his heart isn't made of gold. As a matter of fact, his heart isn't even the color of gold.

"Give me a call when all of you are ready," Eileen said, already pressing a button to take another call. The office phones had been ringing nonstop with concerned residents. Honestly, it was one of the reasons I loved this town. She gestured toward the boxes of hand warmers that were stacked into a tower before speaking into the receiver. "Paramour Bay Sheriff's Office. How may I help you?"

I grabbed the top box, which was still half full, for the group I was about to assemble. I waved goodbye to Eileen, fully expecting to see her later. I was wishing I'd opened a package of them when I stepped outside. The freezing temperature stole my breath and also caused my skin to feel like brittle china. I couldn't wait to change into multiple layers, tucking some of these hand warmers in a few very discreet places.

I so didn't need to see that mental picture.

I meant my pockets.

"You're going to hear a lot more from me if you don't go and fix what you did," I muttered from behind my scarf. "Mom must have asked Ted to do her dirty work, if you get my drift. We'll never get the smell out of him."

Leo began to hack, but it wasn't to throw up a hairball. It was the sound of his belly laugh when he'd caught sight of Ted strolling down the sidewalk with a pair of long yellow rubber gloves.

"It's not funny, Leo. And why would Ted agree to such a thing?"

You see, Ted and my mother weren't what you would call

close. Nan had created Ted around eleven years ago to keep her company, as well as to help her obtain material components for more complicated spells. He lived in—

Shed, Raven. Tell the truth. It's a Ted Shed. Now that I think about it, it's more of a shack, really.

By this time, I'd made my way across the intersection. I'd quickened my step to make sure I could impede Ted's access to town square. There was no way I was allowing him to dig through…my gag reflex kicked in.

Leo started with that hacking laugh of his once again.

Anyway, Ted lived on the back of my property behind my cottage. Nan had acquired him from the wax museum located at on the front end of town. Technically, he was built to resemble Lurch from "The Addams Family". He was literally six feet six inches, whitish-blond hair, crooked teeth, and had a penchant for wearing suits styled in the late 1800s. He was unique, and everyone adored him.

"Ted," I called out, lifting my chin up so that my lips were no longer covered by my scarf. I wanted him to be able to hear me. "Ted!"

Ted had stopped in front of the display window of Mindy's boutique. He was waving, but not to Mindy. There was a mannequin inside that he had fallen head over heels in love with, and I knew there would come a day when he would no longer be satisfied with simple waves or even helping Mindy around the store. She didn't mind the extra help reaching some of the higher racks, plus she thought it was just a quirk that Ted seemed to adore one specific mannequin over another.

You're getting warmer.

No, I wasn't, but that was here nor there.

"Ted, what are you doing with those gloves?" I asked, already knowing the answer. Still, I couldn't believe my mother could talk him into such a disgusting chore. "Don't answer that. Give me those."

"I am helping Ms. Regina."

"This is the third or fourth time that you've done something my mother has asked of you, Ted." I set the yellow gloves on top of the box of hand warmers. "Since when have you and my mother ever seen eye to eye?"

Are your pockets warm yet?

"I'm not warm, Leo. I'm freezing," I announced, stomping my knee-high dress boots to keep what heat I had left moving through my body. "I'll give you a ride back to the house, Ted. I was hoping that you'd join Heidi, Mom, and me in a group to search for the missing reindeer."

"I need to go to the town square," Ted stated matter-of-factly. Since he was a wax golem, he was rather concise with his replies.

"No, you really don't," I stressed, scrunching my nose in disgust. "Mom was going to have you sift through piles of caribou excrement, Ted. She was tricking you, and you somehow fell for it."

"It's okay, Miss Raven. I want to help."

Ted gave that eerie smile of his, where his chipped front teeth showed in an uneven display. His gaze of adoration was like a laser beam, focusing on the mannequin wearing the cutest outfit I'd seen this season. I made a mental note to keep track of when Mindy put the pieces on sale. It was in that moment that I realized what I'd been missing these past couple of months.

Hot dog! Scorching hot, and it only took you two months, one week, and two days to figure it out. I had a bet with your mother. Now she owes me twenty bucks.

"Ted, please tell me that Mom didn't promise to bring the mannequin to life if you helped her out," I pleaded, not able to deal with another golem at the moment. It was bad enough that the town of Paramour Bay had a local grim reaper named Ivan, a werewolf librarian named Harry, Rye, myself, and Ted. I'd known that adding my mother into the mix was like striking a match to see how much powder was left inside the keg, but for her to go so far as to bribe my companion? "Ted, you know that those types of spells could have consequences."

"Ms. Regina's offer was far too tempting."

The Mistress of the Dark did sweeten the deal with giving the mannequin dimples. Face it, Raven. Your mother is the queen of manipulating the weak.

"Not this time," I muttered, disappointed in all three of them. I ushered Ted to my car before icicles formed on the end of my nose. "Leo, I expected this type of thing from Mom. But you? I can't believe that you didn't tell me about this when you figured it out. You even bet on when I'd figure it out on my own!"

"Leo only found out today," Ted said, attempting to save my familiar from being thrown under the bus.

I made the bet in your favor, so that should count for something. And the only one driving a bus around here is your mother. Unfortunately, we're just the hapless passengers.

"Not true," I denied, having made it clear to Mom that she didn't get to waltz back into town as if she owned the place. "I'm the driver, and you left me blind to what was going on. And Ted, I promise the next time that Mercury goes into retrograde that we'll cast an animation spell to animate your friend."

Uh, Raven? We haven't covered that particular incantation in our lessons yet.

"The next time Mercury is in retrograde is in mid-February."
I unlocked my old Corolla after having had to go back for Ted
when he'd turned around to wave to his love one more time.
"We have time to go over lesson plans. Right now, we need to
save a reindeer before he is mistaken by some hunter as a mule
deer."

*Since when did it fall on our shoulders to save Christmas? You
realize that Senile Santa isn't the real deal, right? I'm telling you
that he was recruited by Skippy's agents of evil. Now that your
mother has lost our bet, I'm going to call in my favor—a truth spell
on Fake Father Christmas himself.*

"We talked about privacy, Leo. We're not using a truth divi-
nation on anyone, especially a man who's giving his time so that
the children in Paramour Bay continue to believe in the spirit of
Christmas."

I'd already opened the driver's side door, storing the hand
warmers and yellow gloves in the backseat. Ted was busy
pushing back the passenger seat to accommodate his long legs,
while Leo suddenly appeared on mine behind the steering wheel
right when I'd been about to sit. His left eye was focused solely
on the windshield. I followed his gaze, which had landed on a
red envelope that had been tucked underneath the wiper blade.

Don't touch it, Raven. Try to learn from past mistakes.

"It's not like I can drive with an envelope stuck to my windshield, Leo," I muttered through my chattering teeth. I quickly
snagged the note and shooed Leo into the backseat. "Let me
warm up the car first."

It took three attempts, but the engine in my old Corolla
finally turned over. Just last month, Newt had worked on the
heater to ensure that I could make it through another winter.
The best part was that he hadn't even charged me labor, saying

that it was his Christmas gift to me.

That's just because the talking lizard wants a discount at the shop.

"That's not true," I argued, managing to open the envelope while my hands shook from the cold. I'd taken my gloves off in the police station and tucked them in my jacket. "Newt doesn't even drink tea. Now, who would leave us a note?"

No one, which is why you shouldn't have touched it…and with your bare hands. What good is it to watch "NCIS" if you don't pick up on what not to do at a crime scene?

"My car isn't a crime scene, Leo," I said, sliding out what appeared to be a stock card of some sort. The material was thicker than paper, almost like those holiday cards with pictures printed on them. "I think this is just a Christmas card from one of the shop—"

Keep going. Finish your sentence. Better yet, don't. Slide whatever it is that you pulled out of that envelope right back in, and we'll forget this ever happened. Hey, tell Ted to shift one of those vents my way. We wouldn't want him to melt on the way home, now would we?

"Leo?"

Don't Leo me, unless it's to tell me that we have the day off and a pile of properly aged Honduran organic catnip ready for my pipe. Then you can Leo me all you want.

"It's a message from…Santa Claus."

That's it. I'm returning your present that is already wrapped underneath the Christmas tree and buying you a pair of hearing aids.

Chapter Four

"**H**AVE YOU CONSIDERED that this Santa Claus imposter is working for either the coven's governing council or possibly even Aunt Rowena's breakaway faction?"

Your mother has no idea what she's talking about. She must be drinking again. We've already established that the Santa Claus in town square has been conned to do some job by Skippy's nefarious minions.

I was currently in the kitchen, topping off my thermos with some select one hundred percent Columbian coffee that I'd brewed while changing out of my work clothes. Life had its challenges, but there was no need to settle for cheap coffee when I owned the only premium tea and coffee outlet in town.

Now that I was dressed properly, the multiple layers would keep me warm while out and about today, though I did plan on cruising in the warm car when possible. The roads were clear enough that my old Corolla would do just fine, although there was a stormfront on the horizon for next week. What I really wanted for Christmas was a new Jeep Wrangler, one with a hard top and four-wheel drive. It was hard enough getting around in these cold Northeastern winters without the added heartache of a troublesome vehicle.

"The two of you always assume the worst," I said, twisting the cap of the thermos into place. "I had been hoping that the

Santa Claus the town council hired was also part owner of the petting zoo. Liam texted me a bit ago, confirming that Barry Mina owns the petting zoo with his cousin. Maybe the cousin took the Santa Claus job, which would explain his initial concern about losing one of the animals from their main attraction."

Then Skippy managed to rope in both cousins with the promise of unending acorns, because how else would you explain their knowledge of Crayolahead's existence?

"Leo does have a point," my mother said, laying the envelope and note on the counter. She gestured toward the letter and relayed the message. "*Thank you for helping save Christmas. Yours truly, Santa Claus.*"

My mother had shown up to the cottage a few moments ago, decked out in what appeared to be a form-fitting black ski suit and one of those hats that had a hole in the top for a ponytail to stick through. She must have made the opening larger to accommodate the massive pile of black hair she always firmly secured on top of her head. She declared herself ready to join the search for the missing reindeer, though she'd stated her reservations about there even being a mystery to be solved.

"Then again, Leo always overdramatizes these occasions."

Where's a snowball when I need one? I'd settle for a falling icicle right about now.

"Barry or his cousin probably saw me go into the police station," I theorized, not able to bring myself to believe that the man dressed as Santa Claus was anything other than someone who wanted to brighten the season for the children of Paramour Bay. I'm not saying that the note wasn't unusual, but that was becoming quite the norm here in Paramour Bay. "I'm also usually on the other end of an overactive imagination, though not quite as bad as the two of you. Mom, you've been seeing magical conspiracy theories ever since our run-in with Aunt Rowena at the graveyard. And Leo, you're in a funk all because Skippy and his friends have gone into hibernation. The two of you really need to get a grip on yourselves and start a hobby to occupy your time."

What I need is a couple puffs off my pipe before we wander around out there in the frigid outdoors. I read an article in Catnip Aficionado that premium organic catnip helps regulate the body's temperature more effectively. I hope you don't mind. I subscribed to another annual subscription. I couldn't pass up the half-price offer if I renewed it early.

"We shouldn't underestimate Aunt Rowena," my mother warned with a shake of her finger. "Nor Rye. Are you sure that Santa Claus didn't look a little familiar?"

"No, Mom. I'm fairly positive that Rye didn't go to all that trouble to dress up as Kris Kringle just to talk to me in some annoying cryptic fashion."

For once, I sounded like the only adult in the room. I'll be honest and tell you that it was rather gratifying. I was even going to take my newfound independence a step further. There were some unresolved issues that needed to be agreed upon if we were all going to trust one another.

"Mother, you were seriously in the wrong to blackmail Ted into helping you this past month," I chastised, carefully setting the empty coffee pot into the sink to wash later. "You played on his feeling of admiration for that mannequin—"

"Beth."

Sweet angel of mercy, the grey candlestick has gone and given the plastic doll a name. I'm putting my paw down if those two decide they want a kid. With my luck, it'll be made of metal.

I must admit, Ted had thrown me off my mature train of logic. We all stopped talking and stared at him, where he was waiting for us by the door. He immediately displayed one of those straight, endearing smiles of his. My heart fluttered at the romance of it all. He'd given his beloved mannequin a name. How could I not follow through with my promise now?

Only you would somehow chalk up giving a mannequin a name as romantic. Others would be calling an ambulance to take him straight to the loony bin.

"You played on Ted's feelings for Beth," I amended, not happy that my mother had chosen such a devious route. "That was underhanded and uncalled for. We're a team, Mom. It's how we've worked in the past, it's how we get things done, and it's how things are going to stay as long as I have anything to say about it."

I think I like this side of you, Raven. Go ahead and take charge. That way, there's someone to blame when this whole thing blows up.

"Leo, you should probably know now that I told Mindy we'd watch Cupcake when she went on vacation in January," I said, not knowing how much longer I could keep that news to myself when Leo was pretty much privy to every single thought in my head. She'd called last Wednesday when Leo had been at his weekly poker game, and I had used an itsy-bitsy spell to camouflage my memory from him. The magical influence of the elements I'd drawn on had been bound to weaken sooner or later. "Leo?"

A quick glance over the island and across the living room/dining room area where Leo had curled up on his bed revealed that his whiskers were twitching every which away upon hearing my announcement. Well, he'd just have to get over it. These were the things we do for friends, and Mindy's small request revealed her trust in me.

"It's only for four days while she and Larry take a long weekend for themselves," I stressed, needing Leo to be on board with the whole cat-sitting thing.

"Ted was helping me out on a few things," my mother defended herself. She'd been sitting on one of the stools at the counter, but she was presently making her way to where Ted awaited us by the door. "He does it for you all the time. Right, Ted?"

"Ted was Nan's companion, just as he is mine. He was never yours." I grabbed my thermos and made my way around the island. We were waiting for Heidi to join us before heading out with a planned route. "He wasn't created to do your bidding. He's got a mind of his own, a heart full of affection, and loyalty to the Marigold family. We should cherish him, not abuse him with demeaning chores."

You're right, Raven. We should cherish the gifts in our lives, and I'm going to start by getting into the spirit of the season. I won't let news of Cupcake's impending visit ruin my holiday. As a matter of fact, I'm going to use the upcoming visit as a way to sharpen my mentoring skills.

I was afraid to ask Leo why he'd taken on such a bright and cheery attitude. For once, I ignored his confusing insight and focused on my mother.

Then it hit me.

"Leo, you cannot use Cupcake as cannon fodder in your ongoing battle with the local squirrels."

Who, me? The thought never crossed my mind more than once or twice.

I would have to come back around to that conversation before Cupcake's visit. Right now, my mother was the loose cannon we needed to contain.

"I'm serious, Mom. We do things as a team, and Ted is now his own person. He's a member of the team by his own choice. I made him a promise to utilize a transformation spell on Beth when Mercury goes into retrograde this coming February. If you want to be part of this team, then you can help make sure that we get the spell done right. After all, you made him a promise to bring Beth to life, too."

"Fine," my mother said in acquiesce, though she appeared a bit put off that I'd taken away her leverage. "Let's just see to finding this missing reindeer, shall we? Although I must say that you're making it difficult by not collecting those samples we needed from the petting zoo in town square."

"Who needs those types of samples when we have Leo?" Heidi exclaimed, having caught the tail end of our conversation. She was dressed similarly to my mother, although Heidi's winter outfit was baby blue to match the color of her eyes. Her blonde curls were tucked into a ski cap while her gloves were hooked to a small belt attached to her waist. "Look! Aren't these the cutest things ever?"

Raven, for the love of all things magical, do something before my beloved Heidi takes another step closer with those...what in Hades are those things?

"Leo, I present to you these tiny Ugg winter booties," Heidi exclaimed, kicking off the snow she'd tracked in on the interior welcome mat. It didn't take her long to slide her fuzzy socked feet out of her boots. "This way, your paws stay nice and dry on our search."

Leo's minor weight problem prevented him from scurrying down off his bed before Heidi reached his location with her collection of four tiny insulated high-top moccasins. I definitely gave her credit for being quick on the draw, because it was only mere seconds before Leo's paws were covered with matching leather booties. Heidi lifted him down off the windowsill so that he could try them out.

My mother's fit of laughter until she was wiping the tears from her eyes didn't help Leo maintain any dignity. He was lifting each foot as if he were wading in water, causing Heidi to clap in excitement.

"See? Don't they look and feel great? They're actually made for babies. What do you think?" Heidi asked with a smile, unable to hear all the inappropriate words that my mother and I were catching in between Leo's questioning of his judgement on women. "Are we ready? Let me grab the oatmeal. Oh, and I can't wait to tell you all about my meeting with Cora. I now have her wrapped around my little pinky."

"Oatmeal?" I held up the thermos full of coffee in confusion, deciding to pass on the Cora conversation. The less I knew about that woman, the better. "I have everything we need right here, unless you didn't eat breakfast. In that case, oatmeal will take way too long. Just grab one of those breakfast bars that I have in the pantry."

Tell her to grab the scissors while she's at it, because I am not going out dressed like this. Look at me, Raven. I look like I've gone native with these things strapped to my paws.

My mother went into another fit of laughter, leaning against Ted so that she didn't fall over. He didn't look amused, and he was probably still a bit peeved once he realized that she'd been blackmailing him with empty promises this entire time.

"The oatmeal isn't to eat, Raven," Heidi explained, walking past me and into the kitchen. "You see, my dad used to take me fishing in the summer. He always stressed the importance of having the right bait. The same scenario applies here."

Pocahontas? If memory serves me correctly, reindeer don't care for cats dressed as Native Americans…it's cultural misappropriation, that's what it is. Forcing me to walk around in four child-sized moccasin booties will get us nowhere.

"You better leave the oatmeal and grab whatever sugar cookies we have in the pantry," I warned her, thinking about what could very well be the reason Randy had wandered off on his own. "Bobby Hurst was feeding him reindeer his sugar cookies instead of what was being provided by the petting zoo. I thought we could swing by Bobby's place first."

"Why don't I take Ted, and we can—"

"Not a chance," I said, interrupting whatever my mother had been about to say regarding sneaking off with Ted. "Mom, you're coming with me where I can keep an eye on you. Heidi and Ted can take her car, allowing us to split up and cover more ground. We'll use our phones to text updates to one another."

Speaking of phones, mine vibrated in my snow pants. I wasn't wearing the formfitting style that my mother had on, but instead I was sporting one of those puffy, not-so-stylish pants that made my lower half appear as if it belonged to an abominable snowman. They weren't nearly as cute, but they were definitely practical.

"It's Liam," I murmured, swiping the button on the display so that I could read his message. My stomach did that pivot move that sent it directly into a nosedive. "Barry Mina's cousin is currently spending the holidays in North Carolina with his wife's family. It turns out that he wasn't the Santa Claus from last night, after all."

"Raven, dear, I don't understand what all the fuss is with this Santa Claus," my mother said, waving her hand in the air as if I were making a mountain out of a molehill. She then grabbed her black leather gloves from the entryway table and pointed them my way. "You clearly haven't spent enough time around those displays to know that the actor does his best to get into character. I once volunteered as an elf when you were either three or four years old. Trust me, the man playing Santa Claus probably thought you seemed nice and wanted to impress you with his acting chops. Happens all the time. Relax."

"So," Heidi exclaimed, coming up to stand beside me with a container of oatmeal in one hand and a package of iced sugar cookies in the other. "Where does that leave us?"

I shot my mother a warning glare when she would have undoubtedly said that this news led us directly back to the petting zoo in town square. We were *not* sifting through piles of dung.

"We stick to the original plan and start canvassing the neighborhoods. You and Ted take the main part of town, while Mom and I will take a peek around Bobby Hurst's residence for any sign of hoofprints."

Speaking of prints…

Leo hadn't piped in with his one-line zingers lately. Heidi seemed to notice that, as well. We both began looking for him, which shouldn't have been difficult given that he was basically wearing leather hip waders on each paw. Mom and Ted were looking somewhere behind us, with my mother's smile widening with humor.

"Leo, those paw protectors were expensive." Heidi raised the items in her hands in defeat, staring at Leo in disappointment. He was licking his front paw in satisfaction of a job well done, having gnawed through them in record time. "How did you get them off, and what did you do with them?"

From Leo's satisfied squint and the way he sat back so regally, which wasn't an easy feat, my bet was that he'd stuffed them down the garbage disposal after pulling them off.

I've come to find out that there are just some things that I won't do for love, Raven. Being humiliated is one of them, no matter how much I adore my beloved Heidi. Now, what did I miss?

Chapter Five

"I'M SURE THAT the poor reindeer just wanted to get home," Wilma said with a frown. She puttered around in her kitchen, cleaning up the dishes from her lunch. "Did you know that Alaska has caribou, as do some provinces in Canada? Maybe he's wandered off in search of cooler weather."

I'd done some research while searching for Randy, and the petting zoo was actually made for wild animals who could no longer survive in the wild due to some incapacity. Barry and Joel Mina had created the refuge initially for bears, using their family's farm as a sanctuary after finding an injured black bear cub on their property that the mother had abandoned. Upon realizing that the cub would never survive on its own, one thing led to another until word had spread about their undertaking. Eventually, the operation grew into a nonprofit organization with the sole purpose of becoming a full-fledged sanctuary.

"Actually, the reindeer in question is quite domesticated," I repeated for the third time this morning. Technically, it was a little after twelve. My stomach grumbled at the delicious scent of pasta. Wilma must have heated up some leftovers, as I didn't see any of the pans required to prepare such a meal in the dish rack. "The owners of the sanctuary call him Randy, and he's one of nine other reindeer who somehow ended up on their farm for one reason or another. No one knows for certain what happened to them or how they came to be in Connecticut, but they can't go back to the wild due to their domestication. They've become dependent on Barry and Joel to survive."

The reason for my repeated conversations was that everyone had assumed that the caribous in question were being used to turn a pretty penny for the refuge. In reality, those reindeer thrived on being around people. They craved the attention of humans, and they'd come to associate them as providers and protectors. Yes, it was strange, but it was indicative of adaptive behavior. Since it wasn't the norm when it came to those types of beautiful herd animals, they couldn't be released back into the wild. But the Minas had found out early on that the reindeer wanted to be around the comforting influence of humans.

This search is pointless, Raven. Any tracks that the antlered brute left behind were covered with a fresh dusting of snow last night. I say we head back to the tea shop where we can all indulge in our favorite addictions, and take the rest of the day to contemplate our own fragile existence. I can only take so much of being cooped up in your rolling death trap. Add in the oh-so-very special company of your mother, and I'm ready to take a hit off the tail pipe. It's like being sealed inside a cardboard box with a swarm of annoying wasps.

The new layer of snow wasn't even a half inch, so I didn't buy that we couldn't track Randy if we came across his path. The problem was that the town square had been kept clear enough for the festivities. Randy could have easily kept walking on the road without leaving a trail for miles. As for any piles of steaming brownies left in the streets, I'm relatively sure they would have been run over by vehicles enough times that there was nothing left to find.

Don't even consider it, Raven. We are not driving miles out of town on the side of the road in search of tracks that wouldn't be visible without getting out of the warmth of the car. Do you know how long that would take? We'd all die from pneumonia before we made it back home.

One didn't get pneumonia from being outside in the cold weather when you were dressed properly. On top of that, we'd be able to make do with a pair of binoculars…not that I owned a pair.

See? Discussion over. I'll go let your mother know that our special allotment of bonding time is over.

"I'm sure that the reindeer is fine wherever he's gotten off to," Wilma declared with a nod. She wiped her hands on a dishtowel. "I'm on my way over to Elsie's house, but I'll call Eileen should I see anything out of the ordinary. Did you know that Elsie still can't find her favorite pair of reading glasses? She's been driving me crazy these past two days."

"I can pick her up a pair from the boutique," I offered, knowing Mindy kept a stand of eclectic reading glasses in almost every color. A hot flash washed over me, mostly because I was still wearing my snowsuit in a house that had to have been set to eighty degrees. "Mindy is having a holiday sale. Two for the price of one."

"I tried that," Wilma complained, clearly irritated with her best friend. She shooed me through her kitchen and into the living room. "I even bought Elsie those pink ones that she's been eyeing for the last month. All I hear is that her old ones fit perfectly over her hearing aids, and the new ones don't feel nearly as comfortable."

Wilma's phone rang, causing her to detour to the side table next to the couch. She still had a landline, which proved that she was very set in her ways. As a matter of fact, I wasn't sure that either she or Elsie owned a cell phone.

"I was just about to put on my coat," Wilma said into the receiver. Right at that moment, someone knocked on the door. She sighed in irritation. "Elsie, hold on a second. Someone's at the door."

The fact that Wilma wasn't getting to watch her afternoon soap operas was definitely wreaking havoc on her day. Seeing as I'd managed to put my boots back on while she'd been on the phone, I stood up and answered the door for her.

Wilma and I both jumped when the local school cheerleaders began to belt out an overwhelming loud rendition of "Silent Night", one of them holding a basket for donations. I'd heard that they were caroling this year to raise money for new uniforms. It was a good thing that I'd stuffed a few dollar bills into my coat pocket.

"I've got your back, Wilma," I said after the girls had finished singing, figuring it was time for me to head out anyway. We still had a few houses to visit in hopes that someone saw something, though we'd probably still end up going for a drive on the outskirts of town in search of hoofprints. "Go talk to Elsie. Just remember, call Eileen if you see Randy anywhere."

Wilma thanked me, though she was muttering something about her soap opera as she closed the door behind me. My mother had stopped the girls before they began to veer down the sidewalk to the next house, asking if they'd seen the missing reindeer. They all claimed that they were keeping their eye out for him as they caroled throughout the neighborhoods, which just solidified our next step.

"We need a set of binoculars, Mom."

No, we don't. We already agreed to a staycation involving a fresh pipe filled with Honduran Organic catnip for the remainder of the day, remember?

"You're the only one who agreed to that idea, and Mom and I are vetoing you and your pipe." I leaned back against my car as I thought over our options. "We do need to eat lunch, though."

I'll take what I can get, but I want a nap thrown in there somewhere.

"What about a drone?" my mother asked, joining me against the car. She crossed her arms in thought. "Does that handsome sheriff of yours own one of those high-tech drone-copters?"

The only way we're using a drone is if I can attach your mother to it and drop her somewhere out over the bay.

"You're just being a sore loser," my mother countered with a Cheshire grin. She was about to hit below the belt. "You lost yet another epic battle against the same furry-tailed rat this past fall. It happens to the best of us...not."

"Mom," I warned, not needing another battle to ensue right in front of me. "Let's get back to this idea of yours. I don't think Liam has one of those drones, but your idea is brilliant."

Great. Inflate her ego even more. She can float away on her own, and then we won't need the drone after all.

The longer I thought about it, the more I realized how ingenious it was. How easy would it be to scour the town of Paramour Bay from the air? We could locate Randy in no time, even if he was in someone's backyard.

The sound of an engine caught our attention. We turned in time to see Karen Finley pulling her husband's vehicle into their driveway. Granted, it was pretty darned cold outside, but she got out of her vehicle with a brown paper bag in hand and made a beeline straight to her front door without even a wave.

"That was odd," I murmured, still staring at Otis and Karen's house in contemplation. "It's not like Karen to ignore anyone."

You forget that your mother is in our presence. She's—

I tapped on the window with my glove, pointing a finger in warning at where Leo sat in the backseat of my car all toasty warm since I'd left the engine running. Newt had done a fantastic job with the heater.

"Stick to one mystery at a time, Raven," my mother said, gesturing for me to move away from the passenger side door. "It's time for lunch. I'll take a sandwich over to Beetle after we're done while you figure out who has a drone we can borrow."

I wasn't sure it was going to be that easy of a feat, but I did agree that it was lunchtime. We'd searched several backyards upon spotting disturbances in the numerous snow-blanketed front yards, but all explorations had proved worthless. On the bright side, I'm relatively sure that I hit my exercise quota for the month.

It didn't take me long to settle in behind the steering wheel, taking a moment to let the heat from the vent warm up my cold cheeks. I had already pressed on the brake and was just about to switch gears when a flash of blue caught my eye.

"Well, what do we have here," my mother murmured, our gazes following one Bobby Hurst. He'd come running in between houses about four driveways down from where we were parked. He was in such a hurry that he didn't even look both ways before crossing the street. It didn't take him long to disappear behind the houses on the opposite side. "Leo, you're up."

Why me? In case you've forgotten, I got rid of those mukluks your bestie attempted to strap on me, and now my paws are exposed to the harsh elements. You wouldn't want me to get frostbite on my tootsies, would you?

"Don't answer that," I warned my mother, thinking it might have been a better idea to have allowed Ted to oversee the tea shop while Beetle had accompanied my mother on their own search. I was spending more time being a referee than I was searching for Randy. "Leo, you stay here and keep watch on the Finley's house. I still find it odd that she didn't acknowledge us. Mom, you and I will follow Bobby."

"Seriously, Raven," my mother complained, knowing full well that Bobby was headed for the small patch of woods behind the property lines. "This is why we need a drone. We shouldn't be traipsing around in a batch of trees without the proper colors. What if a hunter mistakes us for deer?"

On second thought, I'll gladly accompany you and take the chance of frostbite. I'm sure the former sheriff's wife just didn't notice you leaning against the car for all the world to see.

"Mom, you know for a fact that there is no hunting allowed back there. It's Paramour Bay's version of a conservation area for the wildlife to roam safely, which is why we should check it out. Liam went to Bobby's house to speak with him and his parents, but what if Bobby took Randy to his treehouse? We'd be negligent not to check it out."

Hey, you don't think that Skippy and his band of ninja misfits were throwing me off their trail by burying acorns around the park, do you? It would be just like them to con me into believing the park was their hibernation area when in actuality...they're in the conservation area! Last one there is a rotten egg!

Leo did his blipping thing, leaving a few black and orange hairs floating in the air while my mother gave me one of her pointed arch stares. I shrugged sheepishly, knowing that she wouldn't allow me to go in the small woods by myself.

"I blame your grandmother for your recklessness." My

mother made sure that her gloves were secure and her hair still perfect before shouldering open the door. "I'm warning you now, Raven. You're cleaning my boots if I step in one of those steaming brownie piles."

Chapter Six

"Is that…"

I let my voice trail off, because I was too afraid to even finish my question. The condensation of my breath dissipated into the cold air. I would have liked nothing better than to do the same.

I'm in full agreement. I'll go first and meet you in the car. You know, to make sure the path is safe.

It actually hadn't taken us that long to cross the street and tromp through the yards in order to reach the small patch of woods. Bobby hadn't been too concerned about leaving his prints in the snow, so the direction he'd taken had been easy to track. The problem we'd encountered had occurred when the palm of my right hand became warm. As a matter of fact, the piercing tingling sensation had me all but crying out in surprise. It was the first time in the last couple of months that my ability to sense when something was wrong had made itself known.

Apparently, I wasn't the only one who had a reaction upon crossing into the foliage. My mother immediately hushed me, nudging me off Bobby's trail and basically in the opposite direction until we'd come upon…an altar.

You read that right, and I'll give you a bit of insight as to why discovering an altar in the middle of a small forest is a very, very bad thing. You see, I'd once visited the coven up in

Windsor during one of our many mysteries. The coven had what you might call a temple, where the witches and warlocks gathered together to show their appreciation for everything the earth provided for them. The scene in front of me was very much the same setup as what I'd witnessed up in Windsor.

"Leo, stay right where you are," I whispered in warning, carefully looking around the large, gnarled oak tree to make sure that we were alone. "Mom, is that what I think it is?"

My mother, who usually had the foresight of caution, didn't hesitate to walk up to the old stone bench that had been positioned in front of the thick trunk. From the couple of inches of snow that rested atop the seat, no one had been here recently. That didn't stop Mom from reaching down to touch the worn limestone, disturbing the thick layer of snow.

The woman has a death wish. I don't know about you, but I only want to interact with Ivan during our weekly poker games. I'm not ready to make that kind of appointment with him, if you know what I mean.

I immediately reached for the special necklace that was tucked away underneath my many layers. Nan had warned me never to be without it, so I understood its importance to my safety. Whatever Aunt Rowena was doing in order to get ready for the brewing war between the factions of the coven, it seemed that she'd brought it here to Paramour Bay.

"We warned her, Mom." I was aghast at the lengths Aunt Rowena would go to in order to involve us in the coven's business. "We can't let this stand. She's spilling over the affairs of the coven without any thought to the safety of these residents. We have to—"

"Raven, it's not what you think."

I see an old limestone bench serving as an altar to Mother Na-

ture. That should speak for itself. You know, come to think of it, I believe I've seen it before.

"You *have* seen it before, Leo."

Mom wasn't the type to get sentimental. Remember, she was the one who'd kept me in the dark about the family secret for thirty years. With that said, every once in a while, I could sense that she missed her old way of life.

Old way of life? In case you hadn't noticed, your mother is every bit as powerful as the Wicked Witch of Windsor.

I had noticed, but I'd chosen not to think about it. Pondering over such evidence only fueled my bitterness toward my mother's decision to keep me in the dark. It had taken exactly one year for me to forgive, accepting that she'd truly believed she had been doing the right thing by me.

Hey, I do remember that bench! Raven, it's all coming back to me! Oh, how I do miss my darling Rosemary.

"Raven, this is where your grandmother came to pay her respects to Mother Nature," my mother announced with a bright smile. "It must be the spot where she would come for a bit of privacy, though I never knew where she snuck off to every now and then. I tried following her one night, but she was very good at covering her tracks. This has to be the place."

Seeing as Leo's memory had been affected by the necromancy spell, it wasn't that much of a surprise that he didn't remember this place. It must have meant a lot to him, though. He was currently rubbing his head on the corner of the limestone bench. My heart broke for him, for he must be missing my grandmother something fierce after recalling such precious moments with her.

Don't get all sappy on me. Clearly, your grandmother is living it up in the afterlife. I have no doubt that she's the one who led us here. I wouldn't put it past her to be the one who caused the antlered brute to go wandering off just so that we would find this special place. Ah, the memories!

"It pains me as usual to agree with Leo," my mother said, gazing up fondly at the old oak tree. The coastal breeze chose that moment to weave its way through the trees, creating a high-pitched eerie whistling sound. "Your grandmother was always the stronger of the two sisters. You should trust in her that she will guide you to the answers you seek."

Why is your mother talking in riddles when this place sounds like the opening of a horror movie? I suddenly have a hankering for one my special edible treats that my BFF carries around in his pocket. This better not be some vessel thing where your grandmother talks through your mother. That malarkey should only be reserved for movies such as The Exorcist. *Great movie, by the way. I just don't want to live through it personally.*

"Leo, don't you have a squirrel to catch?" my mother said with a frown, finally walking back to join me in the spot I'd frozen upon discovering the altar. "Oh, that's right. Skippy won this year's battle, didn't he?"

Never mind. With that wicked tongue, I have no doubt that it's your mother.

"If you truly believe that Nan wanted us to find this place, then why?" I asked, cautiously searching the area for something more than an old bench. "Leo, did Nan ever cast spells out here?"

Not that I recall, but that's not a surprise. What I do remember is that Skippy isn't hibernating in here. He and his gang of ninja misfits got the boot from an old geezer squirrel who didn't like all the commotion. It's the reason Skippy and his minions found new territory over at the park.

"For the love of magic, would you shut your trap?" my mother said, resting a gloved finger against her temple. "Your ramblings are giving me a headache."

While my mother and Leo continued to trade barbs, I warily walked closer to the gnarled and ancient oak tree that must have been over a hundred years old, if not more. I could just picture my grandmother sitting peacefully on the bench while cherishing the great outdoors. I slowly removed my leather glove before gently resting my hand on the old oak tree. Sure enough, it was as if I was touching a warm blanket right out of the dryer. The thick trunk of the old oak was literally humming with a vibrant energy.

"This place is magical," I whispered in awe, wondering how Nan had known this particular tree would be in this very spot. "I know that humans can't feel the energy, but why has no one commented about a limestone bench being found in the middle of these woods?"

"It's not visible to the naked eye, dear," my mother replied matter-of-factly, motioning me back over to her. Leo was still sitting on the small bundle of hay, though it had definitely lost its coloring throughout this past year. "Come. See for yourself."

I'll stay right where I am, thank you. My paws are nice and toasty.

There was something so comfortable about this place that I didn't want to leave quite yet. Unfortunately, we still had a little boy to see about a missing reindeer. My mother was actually stepping back a few paces, still gesturing for me to join her. I was stunned to find that there was an invisible barrier. Once I stepped over it, the bitter cold began to seep into my snowsuit once more.

"I hadn't even noticed the change in temperature," I said,

completely dumbstruck by the discovery. "Wait. Are you saying that Bobby Hurst or anyone else who walks past this place can't see that ancient oak tree?"

Either that, or someone cast a necromancy spell on him...highly doubtful, though.

"Mother Nature has a way of protecting things that she doesn't want to be found," my mother said, motioning for me to turn around. "If you turn quickly enough, you can actually see what others perceive when passing through this area."

I did as my mother instructed. Sure enough, I caught the slightest glimpse of what appeared to be any other tree in this small patch of woods.

Are we done with show and tell? I say the two of you continue on your merry way while I return to keep my BFF some company. I'm sure he's lonely at the tea shop.

"You're with us," I instructed, looking longingly at the ancient oak tree. I'd love to spend more time here, and I would definitely be coming back here to visit. Right now, though, I had a missing reindeer to find. "Let's go and—"

"Oh, dear," my mother whispered, freezing in place before she could even take a step forward.

It's not a deer, Mistress of the Dark. It's only that miniature clown, high on sugar. You know I have a deep-seated fear of clowns.

There was no deer standing right in front us, nor was there a clown. Leo had been referring to Bobby Hurst. Although in Leo's defense, Bobby did resemble a clown with what appeared to be red icing smeared around his mouth. Then again, it could have a fruit drink that stained his upper lip.

Permanently, if you ask me. Have you ever seen that mini-clown without it?

"What are you guys looking at?" Bobby asked with a frown,

peering around us until the tassel of his knit cap tilted to the side. I quickly glanced over my shoulder, still seeing the ancient oak tree. My heart fluttered in my chest. What did he see behind us? "Are you looking for the reindeer? I put a plate of sugar cookies and a glass of milk near my treehouse. I'm going to stay there all day until he decides he's hungry. Then I'll walk him back to the petting zoo so he's not lonely."

Honestly, the antlered brute probably took one look at that mini-clown face and beat hoofs out of town for good. Are you really telling me that little red-stained mouth doesn't freak you out?

"That's very kind of you, young man," my mother said with a smile. She placed her gloved hands on her knees, leaning down so that she was face to face with Bobby. "We're looking the missing reindeer, too. What makes you think that the reindeer would come through here, though?"

I'm just pointing out that your mother's tone sounds like she's luring little girls and boys into a house made of candy. She might be worse than a killer clown.

I couldn't argue with Leo, because my mother's voice was practically dripping with saccharine. Granted, I was now in my thirties. She hadn't really interacted with children in a very long time, and she'd lost her edge.

"You're pretty," Bobby stated off topic with another tilt of his hat, leaving me and Leo speechless. "Would you like a sugar cookie?"

I must be suffering from withdrawal symptoms, Raven. That's the only explanation for that mini-clown's impression of Mistress of the Dark. Either that or he's had way too much sugar this morning. Am I the only one wondering where this kid's parents have gotten off to?

"I'd love one, but we're going to take a break and have

lunch," my mother said, pushing against her knees to stand. "It's good to know that you have this patch of woods covered, though. Thank you for being such a kind person."

"I like reindeer," Bobby said with a single shrug. "Other deer come through here all the time, so why not a reindeer?"

Is this a twist on the old saying about a bear—

"You make a good point, Bobby," I said with admiration after hearing his logic. "Please make sure you tell your parents or the sheriff if you spot the caribou, okay?"

"I have to tell Santa Claus first," Bobby said as he turned around, getting ready to run back to his treehouse.

"Wait, why would you need to tell Santa Claus?" I asked, getting elbowed by my mother so that I didn't put my foot in my mouth. "I mean, Santa Claus knows everything, right?"

Did you just point out that Santa Claus would actually know where all the antlered brutes are at any given moment?

I winced when Leo pointed out my mistake, but Bobby didn't seem to catch my slip.

"I promised Santa when me and my mom were having breakfast this morning," Bobby used his mittens to adjust his knit cap on his forehead. The tassel was so heavy that it kept pulling the material down toward his brow. "Santa came into the bakery for a donut and some hot apple cider. He was getting ready to go out and join the search, too. And you should know that Santa Claus gets his information from all the moms and dads."

I let myself breathe a bit, grateful that Bobby hadn't taken my question the wrong way. Why was Santa Claus joining the search, though, when he didn't even have a stake in the petting zoo?

I say we head back to town so that you can go question the pet-

ting zoo owner, while I go and spend quality time with my BFF.

"And neighbors, I think," Bob said, scrunching his nose in thought. "Santa was talking to Mrs. Finley for a while, too. I couldn't hear what they were saying, but I'm hoping she didn't tell Santa about the time that I rode my bike through her front yard. I left tracks and everything, but it was just because it had rained a lot and I was late for dinner."

Karen Finley? The image of her hurrying into her house without even taking the time to wave to us flashed through my mind. Why had Kris Kringle been talking to Karen? Had we missed something important?

"See ya!"

Bobby took off running, eager to get back to his treehouse to wait for Randy's arrival. Mom and I were left watching him disappear into the woods, both of us knowing what we needed to do now.

I'm not going to get to spend quality time with my BFF today, am I? Raven, you realize that I'm going to have to report you to Santa Claus, right? Your name is definitely going on the naughty list.

Chapter Seven

I T LOOKED AS if I was still on the nice list...at least, temporarily.

Leo ended up getting his wish to spend some quality time with Beetle, because by the time we'd trucked out of the small patch of woods and through some of the yards, Karen Finley had left her house. We'd even knocked on the front door to no avail. We'd had no choice but to drive to the diner after sending a quick text to Heidi that she and Ted should meet us for lunch.

Of course, Ted declined our offer. Instead, he walked over to the boutique to visit Beth, leaving Heidi, my mother, and myself to eat lunch while trying to figure out who owned a drone that we could borrow for the afternoon. We'd also taken a seat by the window, leaving me a somewhat clear view of the festivities that were just getting geared up for the day in town square.

"I texted Liam to see if he knew of anyone who owned a drone," I said before eating the last of my fries. I wiped my fingers with my napkin. "He said that he doesn't know anyone off the top of his head, but he liked the idea so much that he was going to put it into the budget for the sheriff's office at the beginning of the new year."

"I can make that happen," Heidi said with a smile before taking a sip of her soft drink. "I have a meeting with the treasurer next week to go over the town's finances. Hey, I didn't get to tell you about my meeting with Cora."

"Unless that story ends up with her deciding to sell her house and move out of town, I don't want to talk about that woman," my mother said with a grimace, pushing away her plate as if she'd lost her appetite. She'd already eaten her sandwich, though, so the only thing left was part of the crust and the pickle. Who didn't like pickles? I stole it from her plate, not wanting it to go to waste. "Getting back to this missing reindeer, there is one thing we haven't considered."

My mother looked pointedly at me, purposefully casting the Marigold arch of her eyebrow in my direction. We all were very careful not to mention witchcraft in public, just as we were always mindful of how we spoke to Leo when other people were around. Mom was trying to point something out in a manner too obvious for my comfort.

"I'm pretty sure we covered all the angles," I said, hoping that my mother would follow my lead. I even arched my brow in response. "Liam said that he drove a mile outside of town on either side going five miles per hour on the side of the road. He didn't notice any tracks in the snow, but that doesn't mean that the reindeer didn't take one of the back roads. I say we split up, and check on that other lead when we come back to town."

The lead I was referring to was obviously Karen Finley. I'd fully expected to find her at the diner, but she was nowhere to be found. I leaned over until my forehead was pressed against the window, hoping to catch sight of Kris Kringle. I checked the agenda for today's festivities, but the red suit wasn't due to appear until six o'clock this evening. That didn't mean he couldn't put in an earlier appearance. From what Bobby Hurst had said, Santa had been in town earlier talking with a lot of the residents…Karen Finley, in particular.

"I'm talking about Aunt Rowena," my mother murmured, as if I should have known that all along. She craftily held up her coffee cup to hide her lips from anyone watching. "You know…an animal sacrifice."

I'm pretty sure that Heidi's carbonated drink came out of her nose. Unfortunately, her coughing fit garnered almost everyone's attention in the entire diner. Even the cook had leaned out over the counter to make sure that no one was dying.

"She's fine," I called out with a smile, causing Eugene and Albert at the counter to wave their hands back at me. Once Heidi had wiped her nose with a napkin and managed to clean up what had spilled on the table with mine, everyone had pretty much gone back to their own conversations. Once the coast was clear, I shot daggers at my mother. "What is wrong with you, Mother?"

"Oh, don't give me that," she said dismissively. "No one is listening to what we have to say, Raven. Besides, you can't tell me that the thought of Aunt Rowena having something to do with ruining Paramour Bay's Christmas festivities hasn't crossed your mind."

Well, when Mom put it like that…a quick vision of Aunt Rowena holding hands with Krampus strolling down River Bay popped into my mind.

I shifted uncomfortably, leaning back against the padded seat as I thought over the ramifications of my mother's theory. As far as I was aware, Aunt Rowena didn't dabble in dark magic, but she occasionally kept company with some questionable characters.

"I'm telling you now," Heidi whispered fiercely, leaning forward in a spurt of protectiveness. "If that woman so much as hurt a hair on that reindeer's adorable head, I will drive Leo up to Windsor myself and let him have at her with no holds barred."

It appears someone is speaking my language. Tell my beloved Heidi that I've forgiven her for those Jeremiah Johnson throwback boots. I'm locked and loaded on my edibles, so we can hit the road right now. Chop-chop. Time's a wasting. I'll use her floor mats to sharpen my claws en route.

"No one is going anywhere," I murmured, letting Heidi know that Leo had joined the table discussion. It sounded as if he were on the other side of the table, but I couldn't be sure. "Heidi, Aunt Rowena doesn't dabble in that type of magic."

"That we know of," my mother added, finishing off what had to be her lukewarm tea. She set her cup back down on the table before reaching into her purse. "Lunch is my treat. I think while you girls look for the missing reindeer, I'll take a drive up north just to see which way the winds are blowing."

"Mom, I don't think that's a good idea," I hedged, thinking back to the original agreement we made on All Hallows' Eve. "We told Aunt Rowena that we weren't going to have anything to do with the coven war nor takes sides. You can't just go traipsing up to her front door, accusing her of stealing our reindeer for an animal sacrifice."

Actually, I might pay money to see that. Yours, of course, but it would be money well spent.

"Who said anything about ringing the woman's doorbell?" My mother shook her head in incredulity, probably asking herself how she raised such a dramatic daughter. "I'll just take a drive through your grandmother's old neighborhood. If I happen to spot a horse hauler sitting in Aunt Rowena's driveway or large hoofprints and piles of brownies in her yard, then we know she had something to do with this little mystery of ours. If all looks well, I'll be back in time for dinner."

We won't be waiting, if that's what you're wondering.

My mother swiped the check from the table with a roll of her eyes before scooting out of the booth. She reached back for her purse, already having the cash in hand to take up to the register. I couldn't believe that she was actually driving an hour north to ensure that Aunt Rowena hadn't abducted a reindeer for some type of blood ritual.

"Mom, do you know something that you're not telling me?" I whispered warily, grabbing her wrist before she could walk away. "Remember, we promised that we wouldn't keep any more secrets."

And do you recall how well that went? I thought we were on our way to the hospital the night you told her that you'd come clean with Liam about being a witch. As a matter of fact, I'm still not sure she didn't suffer some sort of aneurysm. She must have clutched her head for a good thirty minutes.

"Raven, there is no such thing as being too careful," my mother advised me, patting my hand with the check as if I had no clue how the supernatural realm worked these days. "We're simply keeping an eye on our adversary. It's a wise precaution. Now, I'm going to pay for our meal, tell Beetle that I've decided to drive around to look for the missing reindeer, and grab one of your tea samples from the shop to enjoy on my trip."

Heidi and I exchanged worried glances, knowing full well that my mother's good intentions could vanish as fast as Randy had from the petting zoo last night.

"I'm coming with you, Ms. M," Heidi sighed in resignation. She grabbed her gloves and hat, following my mother's lead, who was already walking toward the front counter. "You owe me, Raven. At least one trip north. They have some amazing outlet malls up that way."

Does this mean I have to stay with you? Heidi can get real feisty really quick, you know. If she spots a trailer or any hoofprints, I'm going to miss all the action.

I began collecting my own winter gear, deciding that I'd stop by the tea shop, too. Once I made sure that Beetle had things covered and didn't need any help, I'd see if I couldn't locate Karen Finley. She had to be somewhere, and there was one person who would no doubt have that information. As for Leo, he was definitely coming with me.

You're planning to use me as bait to lure that antlered brute back into town square, aren't you? You should know that they don't eat cats. They're herbivores, so it's not going to happen, Raven, not even for all the premium organic catnip in the world. Have you seen those pointy spears on their heads? Have you seen my crooked tail? My balance isn't what it used to be. I'd like to keep what's left of my hide intact, thank you very much.

"Hi, fellows," I greeted Eugene and Albert, who were still sitting on their stools at the counter. "You haven't seen Otis, have you? I was hoping he could tell me where to find Karen. I was over at their house, but she wasn't home."

"Otis was with Liam the last time we saw him," Eugene replied, glancing at Albert for confirmation. The older man just nodded his head as he continued to eat his chili. "They were headed into the police station with the mayor when we came into the diner. It's darn cold out there, and we're no closer to finding that reindeer than we were this morning when we started."

"Mom and I went searching that small patch of woods behind Otis' house," I said as I put my hat back on. "No luck, other than little Bobby Hurst putting out some sugar cookies in hopes that the reindeer will show up. I was thinking of driving up and down the side streets leading out of town, maybe even heading over to the lakefront properties to see if they had heard about the search."

Maybe we can pay a visit to the local werewolf librarian while we're over there. Who knows, maybe that card shark knows where the antlered brute has wandered off to. He's got quite the sniffer when it comes to wildlife.

"Were you asking about Karen?" Paula was standing behind the counter with a pot of coffee, refilling the mugs one by one until she stood in front of Eugene. "She was in here earlier, asking if we had any stale bread."

My witchy senses were on high alert, but the palm of my hand didn't warm at the latest news. Wouldn't I experience some sense of energy if Randy were in any true danger?

The fact that you referred to your gift as a witchy sense concerns me greatly, Raven.

"Stale bread?" I began to put on my leather gloves, thinking a stop at the police station was in order before checking on Beetle. Otis had to know where Karen was, right? "Why would Karen want stale bread?"

"She said something about feeding the ducks, though I didn't know there were any this close to town. Last I saw them was near the canals over by waterfront properties," Paula replied with a shrug. "You want a hot cup of tea to go? You'll want something to keep you warm if you're about to go back out there and look for that reindeer. Poor thing. The owner was in this morning and is just beside himself. He said that Randy was the sweetest reindeer of them all."

"Barry was telling us the story of how those reindeer came to be on the farm," Eugene said, picking up his mug that Paula had just refilled with fresh coffee. He rested his elbows on the counter. "It's quite the tale, especially when you have to wonder how nine of them roamed this far south."

Umm, not to give any more credibility to your original theory about the jolly ol' fellow in the red suit...but does that number stick out to you at all?

Nine reindeer? I began singing off the names of those very special ones in the famous song in my mind. Sure enough, there were nine of them. No doubt a coincidence, right?

"I think after this delicious bowl of chili, I'm going to head south," Albert informed us, wiping his mouth with a napkin before patting his belly. "Right to my couch in front of the television, where I can take my afternoon nap. I'm going to leave the search of the missing reindeer to all of you young ones. My arthritis has been acting up, and I'm going to be hurting tonight. Speaking of which, Otis can't say enough about that tea blend you make him every week. You wouldn't happen to have some more of that stuff, would you, Raven?"

Have you thought about raising your prices? The cost of premium catnip...I mean, cost of living and all that.

"I certainly do," I replied, making a mental note to double the next batch of the magical blend I'd become a pro at creating through repetition. I'd certainly come pretty far in my lessons for creating medicinal remedies. That confidence fueled my need for answers to this missing reindeer mystery. There had to be a spell in the family grimoire that could help somehow, some way. "You two have a good day."

Back to this nine reindeer thing...

"I'm in full agreement," I muttered once we were outside. "Do you see what I see?"

Did you hear what I hear? Never mind. That probably went

right over your head. Are you talking about the man who just pulled a truck into the parking space that my beloved Heidi left vacant after she accompanied the Mistress of the Dark on their little holiday mission they might not return from in one piece?

"Don't be so melodramatic. That man parking in front of the tea shop is none other than Barry Mina, the owner of the petting zoo. I recognize him from last night. I think it's time we had a little chat with him ourselves, don't you?"

That was a rhetorical question, right? I thought good ol' Albert had an outstanding idea of how to spend the rest of the afternoon. Hey, where are you going? Gosh darn it, Raven...

Chapter Eight

"MR. MINA?"
I had quickly made my way across the street when I saw that the coast was clear of traffic, not even bothering to use the crosswalk. Believe it or not, a lot of the residents actually obeyed the law, only using the stylized cobblestone walkways that had been beautifully designed and inserted many, many years ago to enhance Paramour Bay's small-town character of a picturesque bayside New England village.

The owner of the petting zoo was dressed for the weather in his salt-stained Carhartt bib overalls, looking exactly like the farmer he was…prepared for Mother Nature's fickle ways. It was easy to tell that he had on more layers than me, and he even had one of those hats with the flaps that came down over his ears.

"Can I help you, miss?"

"I hope so," I replied, falling into step with Barry when it was clear he wasn't going to stop in the middle of the sidewalk. His gaze was trained on town square up ahead. "I helped search for Randy last night, but I was hoping to get a bit more information from you."

"Like what?" Barry shook his head in real concern. "Randy and the others have been with me for many years. He wouldn't just wander away, especially this time of year. He loves these events, meeting new people and all. The others are beside themselves, and they wouldn't even get back into the trailer last night without him. I had to bring more straw out for them so that they'd be comfortable bedding down in the pen overnight."

What's that ache in my heart? I don't like it, Raven. Make it go away. It burns!

Leo was dramatizing, as usual. With that said, my heart hurt for the other reindeer, too. They were worried about their friend, which put a completely different spin on this case.

"Mr. Mina, are you saying that you believe someone took Randy?"

I knew it! There's been a reindeer-napping. This makes all the difference in the world, Raven. I was willing to accept that our horny brute might go out and sow his wild oats, but a reindeer-napping is completely unacceptable. I mean, it could easily have been me they took!

"I explained to Liam that Randy wouldn't just wander off like that, but I can't prove it."

By this time, we'd made it to town square. The winter wonderland was beginning to show signs of life, with a few of the kids taking advantage of their school break to engage in a well-supervised snowball fight. Of course, throwing snowballs at the younger children was considered off limits for even the most competitive among them. They were all busy stockpiling ammunition for what seemed to be an upcoming epic conclusion to their ongoing battle. It seemed that yesterday's snow forts had become massively reinforced and highly complex in their effort to improve their chances of defeating their opponents.

These innocent babes have no idea what it means to suffer through an epic battle. They haven't been exposed to the Machiavellian machinations of Skippy or his band of ninja squirrels yet. I could teach them so much, Raven.

"Did you notice anyone hanging around the pen last night longer than usual? I mean, the gate didn't open itself. You said last night that you are one hundred percent positive that you latched it properly."

"That's the thing of it, miss," Barry said, continuing to walk toward the pen. Sure enough, there were eight beautiful animals all lined up as they waited for Barry. One would assume they were waiting for food, but there was something in their dark eyes that told me otherwise. They were worried about their friend. "Randy knew how to open the latch. They all do. They're very intelligent animals. They survive on their wits in the wild. Among their natural predators are wolves, and they are some of the most ingenious apex predators in the wild. The Norwegian reindeer are very adaptive and watch everything that happens around the herd. I get a lot of hate mail about how I was harming them and that they should be returned to the wild. Unfortunately, there are some rescues that would never survive. They need safe homes—sanctuaries—just like the one we've built. I give them that. I'm not sure why they chose me or my land, but they did. Showed up one day out of the blue, and they've become like my family."

Okay, okay, okay! I can't take anymore, Raven. We'll help. I'll figure out what spell we can use to find that loveable brute, and we'll bring him home where he belongs with his brothers.

I lifted a gloved hand to my lips, not wanting Barry to mistake the meaning behind my smile. Leo did his best to come across as this tough and rough tomcat, but he was just a big old softy underneath. As a matter of fact, he made it appear as if he'd just come around the corner of an outlying snow bunker. His intention to come closer to the reindeer evident, but he was waylaid by a ten-year-old girl who all but screamed in delight at the sight of him.

Uh, Raven?

Leo had stopped dead in his tracks, getting himself into a staring contest with the girl whose older brother was too far away to stop her if she decided to chase after her newfound furry friend. I don't believe I've ever seen Leo's tail puff up to that extent. Well, I'm not counting his reaction to seeing a ghost enjoying a cup of tea in the middle of my tea shop.

Do something, Raven. Now isn't the time to reminisce about our past escapades.

"I'm only here to make sure the others have everything they need before resuming my search," Barry said, drawing my attention his way when I realized that someone else was standing guard at the pen. "Do you know Monty? He was kind enough to stay with the rest of the herd while I went out looking for Randy this morning."

"Hi, Monty," I said, my heart warming at the fact that our community always came together during times of need. "Have you been here all morning?"

Are you seriously going to just stand there and let this little monster come after me? I've changed my mind. I don't want to teach them anything, Raven. They're bloodthirsty creatures, and Skippy and I have an unspoken rule against bloodshed.

I don't want you to think that I would ever leave Leo in a precarious situation. I wouldn't, which is why I kept an eye on the situation while carrying on my conversation with Barry and Monty. Leo was doing a fine job of playing tag. The speed at which he climbed the bunker was quite impressive. I did worry that his short-term memory might fritz out, causing him to disappear in the blink of an eye. It wouldn't do to have the children start spreading rumors about magical kittycats running around town.

"I've been switching on and off with Desmond," Monty said, nodding all-knowingly when he saw my surprise. "I know. He must be in the Christmas spirit. Either that, or Heidi gave him excellent news about his year-end numbers."

Monty took a step back when Leo came darting through the area, followed by the ten-year-old girl with her brother not far behind. Leo's darting was more like one of those headlong sprints of an overweight hedgehog. The attempted turns on the slippery ground were hilarious.

Monsters, I tell you!

"I take it there's no sign of Randy?" Barry asked Monty, already knowing the answer judging by the slump in his shoulders. He let himself into the pen, only to find himself surrounded by the remaining eight reindeer. He leaned down so that he was closer to the head height of all of them. "Hey, fellows. It's okay. I'm doing everything I can."

"Anything on your end?" Monty asked, coming to stand next to me so that Barry couldn't overhear our conversation in case I had bad news. "I saw the mayor go into the police station with Liam a bit ago. They haven't come back out."

"Mom and I were out knocking on doors, hoping that someone had seen or heard something that could help. We even made our way to the small patch of woods behind the Finley's property line, but no such luck. There weren't even any hoofprints in the snow."

Leo was scampering back this way, so I took the opportunity to snag him up into my arms. It probably wasn't the best option for my back, but at least I'd loosened up my muscles by walking around all morning.

"What happened to him?" the girl asked, coming to an abrupt stop in front of me. Her brother came up short, barely running into her. "He looks sort of funny."

Why that little—

I tightened my grip so that Leo wasn't known around town as being a wild, vicious housecat that traumatized small children.

"Maddie, that's not nice," the older brother said, giving me an apologetic smile. "Sorry about that. She loves animals. I'm Josh, by the way. I'm keeping an eye on my sister while my parents help Aunt Candy look for the missing reindeer."

Loves animals? What are those parents teaching these children, Raven? Did you see the ferocious look in that little monster's eyes? And those fools call us feral. It's clear that this she-demon would have wrapped me in holiday paper, slapped a bow on top of my head, and left me to starve to death under some dying Christmas tree!

"This is Leo," I replied, introducing the three of them. I picked up his paw and pretended to wave at them, which wasn't easy considering Leo had gone stiff. "He was a rescue kitty, so he gets a bit scared around strangers when they try to pick him up."

Monty was nice enough not to contradict me. Everyone in town knew Leo, which meant that these siblings were most likely out-of-towners visiting family. I only knew one Candy who resided in Paramour Bay, and that was Candy Hamilton, the owner of our local salon. Leo's left eye was now practically glued to my face. The fact that his one whisker was twitching a million miles per hour told me that he hadn't liked my description of him in the least or the fact that I was indulging in Maddie's wish.

"You rescued him?" Maddie asked before taking off her mitten and stroking her hand down Leo's back. "That was awfully nice of you. I'm going to ask my mom if we can do the same thing. Every pet should have a home."

I know what you're doing, Raven, and it's not going to work. The tiny soft spot in my heart was all taken up after hearing the antlered brute's story. Now send this little monster on her way. If I didn't know any better, I'd say that Skippy was recruiting co-conspirators. First the man in the red suit, and now this she-demon dressed as an innocent little girl.

"You're right," I agreed with Maddie, nodding my head solemnly. "I hope you finally get your kitten, Maddie. I'm sure there's one out there just for you."

"Are you helping Aunt Candy find the missing reindeer?" Maddie asked, still petting Leo. He was purposefully looking over my shoulder as if the girl's touch was unbearable.

I'd take a bear as my new nemesis if it meant this cretin would leave me alone.

"I am," I replied, thinking I'd better cut this short. I wasn't sure how long the mayor and Liam would remain at the police station. Knowing that Otis was with them, I really wanted to find out where Karen had gotten off to this afternoon. "Well, you have fun in your snowball battle."

I need to clarify the bear statement. A black or brown bear would be doable, but not a grizzly. Have you seen the size of their paws? One step is all it would take to flatten me like a pancake. Then it's bye-bye catnip. I can't have that, Raven.

"Maddie, let's go," Josh urged his sister, sending me an apologetic look. "Jade should be here soon. She said she was meeting us here after caroling, remember?"

I do recall Jade being with the cheerleaders singing outside of Wilma's house. Town square was about to get a whole lot busier, but there was still no sign of Santa Claus.

"Here. You can use this." Maddie frowned in concentration

as she unzipped the pocket on her jacket. She reached in, only to pull out a carrot. "I found it last night when everyone was looking for Randy. I was going to feed it to him when he came back, but Mom and Dad made us go home with Aunt Candy."

Is that...is that a baby carrot?

Leo weighed quite a lot, so Monty was kind enough to take the carrot from Maddie. She had no idea that she'd just given us our first real clue that the reindeer hadn't wandered away on his own. Even Barry, who had been listening in on our conversation, began to disengage from the other caribou in order to get closer to confirm Maddie's find.

"Maddie, where did you find this?" I asked, keeping my tone light so that she didn't think she'd done something wrong.

She hadn't done anything, but it would definitely have helped to know that someone had purposefully brought carrots to the petting zoo last night. That wasn't to say an individual hadn't simply wanted to give the reindeer a treat, but Barry had a sign up that warned against offering them such foods. Against popular belief, reindeer actually loved grass. Good old-fashioned green grass, along with various shrubberies, roots, and an occasional mushroom for dessert.

I'd say something about those mushrooms they eat, but I'm not one to talk with my affinity for premium organic catnip. Contrary to reindeer belief, there's nothing wrong with a hallucination a time or two. I wonder if that's how the herd actually ended up on a farm in Connecticut.

Little Bobby Hurst giving Randy a sugar cookie had definitely been a no-no, but that didn't mean another child or even an adult hadn't decided to bring their own treats for the reindeer.

"I found one next to the pen, and the other one in front of Aunt Candy's shop next to the road," Maddie revealed with a simple shrug of her right shoulder. "I got hungry and ate one of them on the way home, but I made sure to save this one for Randy."

I could literally feel Leo's stomach quiver as if his gag reflex had kicked in, and apparently Monty and Barry felt the same. Josh covered his mouth in disgust, all but pushing his sister back to where the epic snowball battle was to commence once the cheerleaders returned from their caroling.

Who in their right mind eats a dirty carrot off the street? If that doesn't prove that she's a street urchin, I don't know what does, Raven.

"I know what you're all thinking," Monty said, switching his contemplative gaze between Barry and me. "Someone could have lured Randy out of the pen with a carrot, but he or she could have also brought the vegetables to give to the reindeer as treats."

"Either way, Liam should know what Maddie discovered," I said, my biceps beginning to cramp from holding Leo for so long. I managed to put him on the ground, albeit ungracefully due to his claws stuck in my coat. "I'll head over to the station. Monty, will you shoot me a text if Randy comes back on his own?"

What are you doing? Don't you dare put me down, Raven. That little monster is still eyeing me like one of those dirty, rotten carrots she consumed without blinking an eye!

"Will do, Raven," Monty replied, checking the time on his watch. "I'll tell Desmond to do the same."

I reversed my course, which took us by the bunkers where more of the teenagers and younger children had gathered for the upcoming battle. One of the volunteer firemen was near the unlit bonfire, stacking brand new wood to the pile in order to have another warm blaze for the pedestrians.

Paramour Bay didn't have street cameras the way New York City did, but that didn't mean one of the shops didn't have their own security cameras. Maybe Candy had one at the salon, not that I'd ever seen one. Nan had never installed one at the tea shop, but she'd placed her own type of protection spell around the perimeter. I understood her reasoning, given that I'd conducted a spell inside a time or two myself. It wouldn't do to have the supernatural caught on video for all the world to see.

You know what this means, don't you?

Leo was still visible to the naked eye, too many people around for him to simply vanish from thin air. He would end up veering away from me at some point, appearing as if he were taking some other route. When he had the opportunity, he would rejoin me in his invisible state.

I feigned adjusting my scarf as we waited at the crosswalk for Newt to drive by, though he was behind the steering wheel of Karen Finley's vehicle. He was clearly taking it for a test drive. That would explain why she'd been using Otis' car this morning, but not why she'd been in such a hurry that she couldn't be bothered to acknowledge me or my mother. It just wasn't Karen's disposition. Had she been the one to lure Randy out of his pen? If so, why?

You're leaving me hanging, Raven. Witches don't do that to their familiar. Let's try again…you know what this means, don't you?

"What does it mean?" I asked, hiding my smile behind my scarf.

I do believe that Paramour Bay has its very first reindeer-napping! The mayor could very well give the key to our small town to whoever returns the antlered brute, which will be me.

"Paramour Bay has a golden key?" I asked, catching sight of

Bob Abbott with an odd-looking wooden whistle hanging around his neck. He was decked out in his hunting gear, though I knew for a fact he'd given up hunting many years ago. It was sweet that he was out here using a caribou whistle to lure Randy back into town. "Who was the last to receive it?"

I have no idea. You know my memory is spotty. Doesn't matter, though. The city could be hiding plans on where Skippy and his band of ninja squirrels hibernate for the winter in the city archives, and that key could unlock the secrets I've been searching for. I don't know why I didn't think of that sooner. Let's get this show on the road, Raven. That reindeer won't find himself!

Chapter Nine

"BARRY MINA DID express his concerns that the reindeer may have been taken out of his pen," Liam said as he set a file on top of his desk. "At this point, it's a tossup whether Randy opened the gate himself or followed a trail of carrots. I'm going to have to deputize you at this rate, Raven. Good work."

Ask the good ol' sheriff about the golden key, Raven. I bet he knows something.

"You can thank Candy's niece," I shared from my seat in one of the guest chairs. Leo had managed to make himself invisible, joining me in Liam's office. Otis had no idea the supernatural existed, so I'd been doing my best to ignore Leo's prompting at every turn. "Her name is Maddie. I'm sure she'd love one of those plastic sheriff badges that you give out to the kids."

Not as much as I'd like that golden key. Besides, that cretin ate a soiled carrot. She doesn't have the common sense to avoid drowning in the rain. She doesn't deserve the distinction that a badge would give her, fake or not.

By the time I'd entered the police station, the mayor had already left to do a photo op with one of the search groups. It didn't surprise me that he would take advantage of this somewhat tragic opportunity, but he really did have Paramour Bay's best interest at heart when the chips were down.

"Well, I better go and join Bob," Otis said, though he didn't make a move to stand from Liam's chair behind the desk. I'm sure he missed the days when he was sheriff, but I'm certain he was proud that Liam had followed in his footsteps. "Bob found an old deer call he had packed away in his garage. We'll take a walk around the town and see if we can't lure that big fellow out from hiding."

Hold down the fort, Raven. I'm going home to see if I can't find something in the spell book to help us win that golden key. Whatever you do, don't solve this case without me. I need that key!

I was glad that Otis didn't seem to be in much of a hurry to join Bob. I still needed to find a way to bring Karen into the conversation, although why she would want to make off with a reindeer was beyond me.

"It won't help if someone took Randy," Liam pointed out, joining me by sitting in the other guest chair. "We just need to figure out a motive. I asked Barry Mina if he had any enemies or maybe any plausible threats for giving those caribou a home."

"And?" Otis asked, his tone favoring that of an active law enforcement officer. He even rested his elbows on the leather armrests of the chair and made a steeple with his fingers in contemplation. "I can imagine that some don't believe that those reindeer can't be reintroduced to the wild. Honestly, Karen and I had this very discussion yesterday before we heard the full story."

I did my best to keep my excitement concealed. This could explain Karen's odd behavior. Had she somehow lured Randy away from the pen using carrots, only to find that her decision to save the caribou had backfired upon hearing that he'd never survive in the wild? Was she trying to figure out how to bring him back without getting caught?

"No threats, no enemies, and Barry Mina was even given a mysterious donation with specific instructions that he or she wanted the money to go toward the upkeep of the reindeer," Liam replied to Otis' inquiry. "As a matter of fact, Mina gets the same donation every year in December."

My right palm kind of tingled, but no heat surfaced from the energy around us. I didn't know what to make of that, so I pushed my curiosity aside to focus on the here and now.

"I saw Newt driving Karen's car when I was walking across the intersection," I said, keeping my eye on Otis. He only nodded his head, even frowning at the inconvenience of whatever had prompted him to take his wife's car to the local mechanic. "I hope it's nothing too expensive. Newt fixed my heater the other day. He sure does know his way around vehicles."

"Might be the carburetor," Otis replied gruffly, his displeasure obvious. "Karen is using my car today to run her errands. Said something about Christmas shopping today, though she already bought my gift. I saw a new fishing pole in the garage behind the water heater, not that she knows that."

"Our secret," I promised with a smile, slowly coming up with a plan that could actually work if someone felt guilty over attempting to help, only to find out that he or she made a mistake. That individual would want to make it right without anyone the wiser, right? "I might have an idea."

I hope it's a good one, because there is no spell we can use that doesn't involve those piles of rancid brownies I tried to get your mother to sort through. I'm still reserving that as our last resort, though I call dibs on being the one to oversee the project. I excel more in a supervisory capacity.

"What's that?" Liam asked, always willing to hear ideas from others. "If you're thinking of offering a reward, I'd have to run that past Mina. Also, it might cause our tip lines to become even busier than they already are…in which case, Eileen might hand in her resignation."

Otis barked out a laugh, most likely because Eileen would never leave Liam in a lurch that way. She loved this town, and she would never give up the reins of answering the phone lines.

"What if we put up signs all over town that basically says he or she can return Randy without any questions asked?" I suggested, waiting for Liam and Otis' reactions. "Think about it. Otis, you and Karen both assumed that the reindeer would be better off in the wild without hearing the facts first. What if someone else thought the same thing, but now regrets his or her decision after hearing Randy's story?"

Want me to sink my claws into the former sheriff's legs? That might get him to confess, if he has any shared complicity with his wife.

Otis was an upstanding man, having once served the town's greater good. I highly doubt that he would have helped his wife abduct a reindeer to prove some point.

Too bad. My claws could use a bit of sharpening.

"That's not a bad idea," Otis said, lowering his arms and leaning forward. "When you think about it, not all of the residents were in town square last night when Mr. Mina was giving an account of how the reindeer ended up at his sanctuary."

"The media is supposed to do a segment on Paramour Bay's winter wonderland tonight. I can have the mayor publicly explain why the herd of reindeer need to remain on Barry Mina's farm, relaying the story over the airwaves," Liam proposed, nodding his approval. "It would also be the perfect time to give the culprit the opportunity to bring Randy back without any questions asked."

Hold the sleigh. Who gets to be the hero then? Who would receive the key to the city?

"You realize that we're basing this on the theory that the reindeer really was abducted, right?" Otis countered, though it wasn't anything we hadn't already covered. "If that poor fellow wandered off on his own, then there's no telling where he got off to last night."

"That's why we'll keep the search groups out for the day before we reevaluate the situation tomorrow morning," Liam said, leaning forward on his chair and turning the base of his office phone to face him. He lifted the receiver and pressed one of the buttons on the side. "I'll run our ideas through the mayor and see if we can't get him on board."

I'm not getting that key, am I?

"Doubt that'll be a problem," Otis said wryly with a twitch of his white mustache. "That man will take publicity any way he can get it. Come on, Raven. I'll walk you out. I'm going to join Bob Abbott's group to see if that caribou thingamabob actually works."

This was my opportunity to talk to Otis about Karen's whereabouts, so I quickly kissed Liam on the cheek and left him wondering why I was in such a hurry to leave. I'd text him later. I did my best to lessen the swooshing sound my ski pants made when I walked, wincing when not even me waddling across the floor as if I was riding a horse diminished the noise.

"Hey, Otis," I called out, trying very hard not to regret my magical tea blend that did wonders for his arthritis. He sure had gotten faster in the last year. "Wait up."

"I thought you were right behind me," Otis said with a frown, not knowing that I'd basically tried to tiptoe out of Liam's office. Eileen was on the phone, telling someone that just because a raccoon had gotten into a garbage can didn't mean that the reindeer would soon be visiting his or her home. "Do you drink that herbal tea you make me? You should, you know. Works miracles."

Leo's hacking laugh echoed in my ears, though I didn't let on in any way that Otis' question had given my familiar fodder for days to come. I realize that turning thirty-one years old two months ago wasn't a milestone, but it was one year closer to my first grey hair.

"Do you know where Karen is right now?" I asked, watching Otis' expression very closely as he held the small swinging door open for me. "I wanted to ask her something about the New Year's Eve celebration at the wax museum."

Why in the world would you even mention that lame party? I'm not going this year. I'm putting my paw down on that one. I'm staying home that night, curling up in front of the fireplace with my pipe, and revising my battle plans for this upcoming spring offensive when Skippy and his ninja squirrels wake up from their hibernation to find their every hope destroyed. I need to be on my game next year. No more nice guy.

I'd heard through the grapevine—basically Wilma and Elsie—that Karen was on the party committee. It served as an excuse as to why I would want to speak with her. Otis seemed to buy it, too, though I did have to push down the guilt that surfaced at my little white lie about my intent.

"Karen is at home, as far as I know," Otis replied, stopping abruptly at the door. I figured maybe a thought had brought him up short, maybe recalling his wife saying something that would explain her odd behavior. But he just wanted to fortify himself against the cold weather outside by adjusting his hat and putting on his thick, insulated gloves. "I had Bob pick me up this morning, though. I didn't want Karen to be at the house without transportation. Do you have her number?"

If there's no golden key to the city, I'm going to head back to the tea shop to hang with my BFF. I didn't get my morning nap in, and trying to keep away from those grubby hands of that street urchin who ate food off the ground has zapped my energy level to below zero. If she consumed a filthy vegetable from the gutter, there's no telling what that little monster is capable of consuming.

"I don't have Karen's number," I said, a spike of adrenaline putting an extra beat in my heart. "I appreciate this, Otis."

Otis waited for me to pull my cell phone out of my coat before rattling off the seven numbers. I quickly entered the information and created a new contact, having every intention of calling Karen the second Otis was out of earshot.

"Thanks again!" I called out after Otis had opened the door, braving the cold temperature as he headed toward town square. "Leo? Come back here right this minute!"

Leo was a no-show, but I didn't want to call Karen while standing in the middle of the sidewalk. I needed to check on Beetle, anyway. It didn't take me long to cross the street at the intersection, taking the opportunity to look for Santa Claus while I was at it. His big chair sat empty.

"...helped Mrs. Salisbury clean up her garbage. She left the lid off again, and those darn raccoons made a mess of things."

"She's always leaving the..."

Two of the men I'd seen with Bob Abbott earlier continued their conversation as they began their walk across the intersection. I'd already made it to the sidewalk, but thought over what they said. Mrs. Salisbury must have been the one on the phone with Eileen. She was a sweet old lady, though she didn't drink tea nor coffee. Rumor had it she liked the taste of Irish whiskey, but I was pretty sure there was no truth behind that chinwag. The only reason I'd met her a time or two was when Liam and I ran into her at the diner.

What if the animal that had gotten into Mrs. Salisbury's garbage wasn't a raccoon? We all made assumptions and disregarded things that were commonplace, but what if we were missing the clues that were being left behind?

The bell rang above the tea shop's door as I entered, and I was pleased to see four customers perusing the sale items. I only recognized two of them from town, which meant the other two were most likely out-of-towners doing some Christmas shopping and enjoying the outdoor festivities in between buying gifts.

Go away. My tummy is full, and I'm settling into catch up on my nap deficiency.

Sure enough, Leo was laying belly up in his bed that was strategically positioned in the display window. Believe it or not, he actually drew a lot of foot traffic in the door. Who didn't love cats?

Mr. Brittle over on Bay Cove Lane, that's who. And for the record, he's not so brittle. His calf is actually quite meaty.

"How's everything going, Beetle?" I asked, though I'm pretty sure I hadn't needed the bell above the door to announce my arrival. There was no missing that irritating swooshing sound coming from my snow pants. "I'm heading out to rejoin the search, but thought I'd stop by to see if you need anything."

"Things are going splendid, Raven!" Beetle exclaimed from behind the counter. His bow tie just so happened to be red and his sweater green. He was the epitome of the holiday spirit. "Just splendid!"

"That's great, Beetle. I appreciate you minding the shop today. I know you were only scheduled for a half day."

Beetle patted me gently on the shoulder as a customer came up to the counter, ready to buy one of the delicate teacups I'd marked down for the holiday sale. I let him do his thing, thankful that he'd finally learned how to input a sale item into the cash register. It had taken a long time to get that system down, but it had been worth every minute.

Don't forget that my BFF deserves a huge Christmas bonus. One that gives him the ability to keep bringing me those premium organic catnip edibles in the shape of Christmas trees. Why are you walking toward me? Raven? What do think you're—hey! Put me down!

"You're coming with me, and this is the only way to ensure that you won't wiggle your way out of it," I muttered after I'd hoisted Leo up into my arms. It wasn't easy with this winter coat, but I'd managed it all the same. "Plus, I know you'd never disappear in front of these lovely customers."

I could sense that Leo was ready to feign the domestic housecat's pain of being picked up and taken out into the cold, so I did the only thing I could—I dangled the carrot. Well, not the carrot that Maddie had forked over, but the taunting carrot that might actually keep Leo from climbing back into his cat bed.

"That raccoon that helped Skippy ruin all your plans this past summer is over at Mrs. Salisbury's house," I said quickly, somehow managing to get the door open without dropping Leo's hefty butt. "Now is your chance to get information that can help you in your upcoming battle with the neighborhood squirrels."

I only got about ten steps when I had to set Leo down on the welcome mat of the local pet shop. It was up in the air if the cold or my exertion was to blame for me being out of breath. Leo had been quiet, which meant he was contemplating my offer.

It's tempting. Underhanded, but tempting. How sure can you be that it's the same raccoon?

"It's the same area where one of the ninja squirrels took you on a detour so that you'd come face to face with the oversized bandit, right?" I hoped I was right. Heidi was off with my mother, Liam was coordinating a ton of efforts in the search of the missing reindeer, and I needed Beetle to mind the shop. Hence, I wanted Leo to keep me company. "I guess I could go find Ted, if he didn't go with Mom and Heidi up to Windsor."

Don't go climbing down the proverbial chimney just yet, Raven. I'm going over my options. And for Jack Frost's sake, would you wave to that old biddy Wilma through the window before she has a heart attack?

I hadn't realized that Wilma was inside the pet shop, which wasn't all that odd. Elsie was always needing paper to line the bottom of her finch's cage, and she'd gone into a funk after losing her reading glasses. It was sweet of Wilma to run errands for her best friend, just as it would be really nice if Leo were to accompany me over to Mrs. Salisbury's residence.

Were you actually trying to guilt me with that thought?

"Look, your options are to either come with me to see about a raccoon or try to avoid another hug from Maddie…who just so happens to be walking this way with her brother," I shared with a bright smile, knowing full well which choice Leo would make.

"Leo!" Maddie called out, running toward us from the other side of the street. Her brother and some of his friends must have taken her to the diner for lunch. It was just my luck that she happened to catch sight of Leo and want another chance to hold him. "Leo!"

Raccoon it is! Let's go, Raven…move it, move it, move it! No time to waste!

Chapter Ten

*I*T'S NOT NICE *to trick your own familiar, Raven. It's in the rulebook somewhere.*

"What rulebook?" I asked distractedly, standing in front of Mrs. Salisbury's house. I'd already taken a look around, but her driveway had been shoveled and salted to perfection with pet friendly deicer. The blue color was a dead giveaway. There was no way of knowing what type of animal had gotten into her garbage. "*Witchcraft for Dummies?*"

They haven't written one for witchcraft. I should know. I checked.

"Maybe it *was* just a run of the mill raccoon that got into her garbage," I muttered, looking back down to the snow that blanketed Mrs. Salisbury's front yard. Whatever critter had decided to go dumpster diving, it hadn't ventured into the main part of the yard. Up near the bay window that most likely looked into her living room was a bird feeder, though. It was easy to tell that the snow had been disturbed in that area, but it was tough to decipher what prints belonged to what animal because the snow had all but been stomped into a thin layer of frozen muck. "You should go around back and see if you can find some raccoon tracks back there."

Oh, now you think a raccoon is responsible. You lured me here under false pretenses. For all we know, a bear could be waiting back there for something better then leftover lasagna. I'd probably be a very tasty morsel, Raven.

Leo was right, and this side trip had been a waste of time. It had been a couple of months since our last mystery, and I was losing my touch. I mean, I actually pondered for a brief moment last night that those nine reindeer might actually be *the* reindeer, and that the man in the red suit had actually been…

Maybe you ingested some of my premium organic catnip before closing up the shop last night. For all we know, my BFF might have left some near the coffee station. It could explain my shortage on yesterday's rations.

"We need to treat this like an abduction," I declared, recalling that Liam had said Barry Mina didn't have any enemies. But didn't everyone? I mean, I considered myself a nice person, but there were still people who probably wouldn't hesitate to deal me wrong. Aunt Rowena immediately sprang to mind. "Barry Mina has to have some type of enemy, like an ex-girlfriend or maybe even someone he declined to do business with. You know, I've heard of corporations wanting to buy the smaller mom and pop farming operations. Maybe Barry turned down an offer and the company hired one of those fixers."

You've been watching reruns of "Law & Order", haven't you?

"Maybe," I conceded, shifting my weight back and forth to keep my blood pumping. The houses lining the street kept most of the coastal winds at bay, but the gusts still seemed to find their way to my location. "Let's do a quick Internet search on Barry Mina and see what we find."

Before I could turn and head back to the car in order to use my phone, the sound of a deadbolt being turned had both Leo and I staring intently at Mrs. Salisbury's front door. Sure enough, there she stood with a firm grip on her cardigan sweater to keep the cold from reaching her neck. It was a good thing that Leo had acted quickly, disappearing in the blink of an eye.

"Are you from Animal Control?"

"No, ma'am," I called out, taking a step forward on the pristine driveway. I'd heard we were getting a few inches of snow in the upcoming days, so it wouldn't be that way for long. "I'm Raven Marigold. We've actually met a few times at the diner. I own the tea shop—*Tea, Leaves, & Eves*."

Mrs. Salisbury tipped her head back and studied me intently through her bifocals.

It wouldn't surprise me if she owned a broom. You know, for the sole purpose of beating furry critters on the head. You don't suppose that this old biddy and old man Brittle have some sort of contest going on between the two of them, do you?

"I'm not senile, missy. I remember you, just as I recall that your grandmother was a bit eccentric. I liked that about her," Mrs. Salisbury stated, as if her opinion of Nan meant that I couldn't be such a bad person. Well, I'd take what I could get at this point. "If you're not with Animal Control, why are you standing on my sidewalk and staring at my house?"

"I was at the station when you called in to speak with Eileen about something getting into your garbage. I just wanted to make sure that it wasn't the reindeer that's gone missing from the petting zoo in town square."

"I said it was a raccoon, didn't I?" Mrs. Salisbury exclaimed in offense. "I called in to make sure that the smell wouldn't attract that antlered brute. The last thing I need is to have that wild animal trampling through my yard and scaring my birds."

If this old biddy didn't rate those feathered pea brains above felines, I would have said we were kindred spirits.

The sound of an engine cut through the neighborhood, and

we all ended up waving at Wilma as she ever-so-slowly drove past Mrs. Salisbury's residence on the way to Elsie's house two doors down.

Whoever it was down at the DMV who gave that woman a license at her age should be fired.

"So, you're saying that you actually saw the raccoon in your garbage can?" I asked, trying not to sound defeated. If I'd known that, I wouldn't have made the trip back through the neighborhood. "You should put the lid on tighter, Mrs. Salisbury. That will keep those sneaky bandits away from the scraps."

"Are you suggesting that I don't know how to handle my own garbage cans, missy?" Mrs. Salisbury shook her finger in my direction in disappointment. "I even put a brick on top to make sure those grubby bandits couldn't make a mess in my driveway. The wind must have blown it over."

I'm not sure that broom-swinging biddy could even pick up a rock, let alone a brick. A broom, on the other hand, weighs in the negatives when she gets that air underneath the bristles.

I had to wonder if Leo didn't have a valid point with the whole brick thing. Mrs. Salisbury couldn't be over a hundred pounds soaking wet. It was highly unlikely that she'd be able to hoist a brick on top of a garbage can.

Another vehicle was passing by, and this time it was none other than Karen Finley. I almost slipped as I quickly stepped off the sidewalk, the road not even remotely as clear as Mrs. Salisbury's sidewalk. I used the hood of my car to keep me upright, but Karen wasn't as slow of a driver as Wilma. Before I could even lift my hand to indicated that I'd like to talk to her, she barreled right on past me.

Mrs. Salisbury could be heard muttering quite the vocabulary for such an elderly woman, slamming the door shut and complaining about the youngins of today's generation. I didn't hesitate, hastily instructing Leo to get into the car. My leather gloves made it a little more difficult to start the engine quickly, but I managed to get my baby going right as Karen took a right turn at the next block.

Are you seriously going to participate in one of those car chases you always see on those television shows? You know that those always end up in some sort of crash, right? I might have to skip this part of the investigation.

"Leo," I called out in warning, sighing in relief when he materialized in the front seat. "You know very well that we're not going to be involved in a car chase. I just want to see where Karen is going. Don't you find it odd that she hasn't waved to a single person today? It's like she's on some type of mission, and it could very well involve Randy."

I still vote to have your mother go through the rancid brown piles of brownies over at the reindeer pen.

I braked at the stop sign, searching for Karen's vehicle. I couldn't see it anywhere, but I waited until I was able to pull onto the street to make sure she wasn't ahead of me. Nope. She was nowhere to be found.

"She had to have pulled into someone's driveway," I insisted, slowing down so that I could check everyone's house. "People don't just disappear."

I could feel the weight of Leo's stare on me, judging my assessment.

"Okay. You can disappear, but regular humans can't do that, Leo."

My phone chimed an incoming message, so I pulled up next to the curb and brought the car to a stop. I scanned the next few houses, but couldn't find a driveway where Karen had parked her husband's vehicle in.

"It's Liam," I muttered, pressing his message to read his text. The implication of his words was not what I was expecting. This couldn't be right, could it? "Um, Leo?"

I heard your thoughts, but I'm going to assume that they got scrambled when you almost slipped back at the broom-swinging biddy's house. Did I miss you hitting your head on the hood of the car or something?

Leo used both paws to look out the front windshield when we heard muffled screams of terror. Sure enough, Bob Abbott was running across the street as fast as his heavy boots would allow, the caribou whistle bouncing against his chest as eight reindeer followed close behind in what I appeared to be a high-speed chase.

Well, that's not something you see every day in Paramour Bay. I hope he didn't use any deer attractant…that could turn out bad for everyone involved!

Chapter Eleven

IT TOOK CLOSE to three hours for Barry Mina to round up the eight reindeer and put them back inside the pen in town square. The hardest part of the whole process had been separating the reindeer from their new friend Bob. He and Otis hadn't counted on the caribou call igniting a fire underneath the eight reindeer, who either thought that Randy was calling out to them from somewhere deep in one of the neighborhoods or a female reindeer was roaming around in heat. Either way, a proper jail break and chase had ensued as a result of Bob's game call.

"I heard that there was a stampede through town today," Heidi said with a chuckle over the phone, still with my mother up in Windsor. Technically, they were just getting on the highway to return home. "I would have loved to have seen that! Beetle immediately called your mother to make sure that she wasn't in harm's way. Isn't that the cutest thing ever?"

Leo began hacking dramatically on a fictitious hairball from his spot in the display window of the tea shop, not finding Heidi's observation cute in the least. On the bright side, he'd finally gotten his afternoon nap and wasn't quite so irritable. I'd spent some time researching Barry Mina more thoroughly, as well as using one of the checks that Karen wrote for Otis' arthritis blend to do a locator spell. Somehow, some way, and by the time I'd gotten around to casting the spell...Karen had made it back home. I'd been about to put my jacket back on, minus the snow pants, and head on over there.

"Beetle is always a gentleman," I replied, glancing over my shoulder. He was currently ringing up a customer, who was talking about all the excitement that had taken place today. "So, what did you find out while you staked out Aunt Rowena's place?"

"Other than she must have had some type of warding spell around her house, nothing."

I took a step closer to the display window, grateful that I no longer had on the snow pants. The warmth of the store had been quite welcoming, and I'd even poured myself a cup of fresh coffee from the carafe. Beetle had done an excellent job in maintaining the sampling tables.

My BFF does an excellent job at almost everything, Raven. Did you see my afternoon treat? It was in the form of a gingerbread man with a beard that was laced with catnip.

Honestly, I'm pretty sure that Leo was envisioning dancing gingerbread men right this minute. That treat of his had been awfully large.

"A warding spell?" I asked, looking up from Leo's relaxed position in the window to see the mayor walk out of the police station. The interview that was set to take place with one of the local news stations was slated for five o'clock in front of Santa's workshop. Town square was becoming quite crowded with residents wanting to be on the news in the background. My plan was to drive over to Karen' house, make sure that she didn't have Randy stashed away in the garage somewhere, and then make it back for the mayor's interview. "You mean, Aunt Rowena knew you were there?"

Ohhhh, do tell. Did the Mistress of the Dark and the Wicked

Witch of Windsor get into an all-out witch fight? I want details.
This has got to be good. Spare me nothing.

"Yep," Heidi quipped, sounding better than I would have thought after having a run-in with my great aunt. "She even invited us inside to have a cup of tea with her. Your mother declined and then drove us off to park on another street."

"Please tell me that my mother didn't have you creeping around people's yards," I pleaded softly, holding the phone closer to my mouth so that no one could overhear me. "Did anyone see you?"

Please tell me that someone turned your mother into a frog. My year would certainly end on a high note in spite of my stalemate with Skippy.

"Just some woman with red hair who came across as if she were from some old Hollywood movie."

I cringed when I realized that Heidi was talking about Angelica, one of the witches on the council. The most cunning, now that I think about it.

"Her name is Angelica," I replied, probably not telling Heidi something she hadn't already discovered after such an encounter. "She's not one we should be messing with, Heidi. She's as shrewd as they come."

Now that I've put more thought into it, allowing your mother to take Heidi up to Windsor probably wasn't the best of ideas. Ask her to put down the visor and look into the mirror. Does she see any whiskers on her face?

"Well, your mother didn't have any trouble going toe to toe with her." Heidi must have moved the phone to speak with my mother, though her words came across as muffled. I couldn't make anything out other than Heidi saying something was fine and that I shouldn't be upset. That was debatable. I could only assume that Mom was trying to downplay whatever she'd said to the Angelica, which set me on edge. "Anyway, there's nothing to worry about. Rowena came outside, got into a rather heated argument with Angelica, and gave me the opportunity to look around the property. No Randy."

A quick glance down at Leo showed that one of his whiskers had begun twitching upon coming to the same conclusion that I'd just come to after Heidi's announcement. There was no mistaking the exclamation of exasperation by my mother, who not so surprisingly snagged the phone out of Heidi's hand.

"Raven, dear, it wasn't quite like it sounds," my mother attempted to reassure me. As a matter of fact, she'd done the opposite. My anxiety level peaked at the thought of Heidi being in danger when we really hadn't had any time to prepare her for such a perilous situation. "Heidi was within my line of sight the entire time. It became apparent that Angelica had been visiting one of the neighbors for the sole purpose of keeping an eye on Aunt Rowena. We inadvertently helped her cause, in a roundabout way, by exposing Angelica's perch."

Come to think of it, the frog spell could have a time delay on it. What coven would want a yard full of frogs all croaking complaints in unison?

I could see where Aunt Rowena might be a tad bit grateful for Mom's inadvertent snooping to reveal such an underhanded move, not that it shouldn't be expected with that particular coven. There was no denying that our family was dysfunctional or that the two factions needed to figure out something out before innocent bystanders got hurt or noticed something that they shouldn't.

"Mom, you promised that you were just going to drive by Aunt Rowena's house to make sure there were no hoofprints or some type of trailer that could be hiding Randy," I pressed her in irritation, reminding her of our previous conversation. I really should have taken this call in the back room, but I hadn't counted on these types of details. "You can't put Heidi in their sights like that. She's exposed."

"By the time Aunt Rowena got through with Angelica, neither one of them cared much about what we were doing there. We quietly left, though I do suspect you'll be receiving a call from Aunt Rowena. Simply explain that we thought she might have broken her promise and that we were checking her out," my mother said, making it seem like such an easy task. "I'll give you back to Heidi. We should be back in time for dinner."

If my beloved Heidi wasn't with the Mistress of the Dark, I'd have you tell your mother to take her time.

Before Heidi could hop back on the phone, I caught a glimpse of red. Sure enough, Santa Claus was walking past Monty's hardware store. I disconnected the line and quickly wove my way through the displays of tea, china, and tables to the back room where I'd left my jacket. I called out to Beetle that he should close up shop around five o'clock and was out the door before I could hear his reply.

If your mission is to speak with the jolly man in the red suit, you're out of luck.

I came to an abrupt halt at the intersection, scanning the sidewalk across the street. There wasn't a Santa Claus in sight.

"Raven, dear, you really should watch where you're going," Cora Barnes complained after I'd almost run into her. The woman was dressed to the nines with a winter coat that cost more than my entire wardrobe. She had on a set of forest green leather gloves that I'd seen in the Coach catalog. They no doubt felt like butter, along with a cashmere scarf that was kept in place with at least a three-carat diamond pin in the shape of a fanciful snowflake. "And for your own sake, put your jacket on before you catch your death in this cold."

I'd only gotten one arm into the padded material thus far. I'd been so focused on locating Santa Claus that I was most likely coming across as scatterbrained, standing in the middle of the sidewalk half-dressed.

Don't feel bad, Raven. An important thought popped into my head earlier before I enjoyed my afternoon edible. I'm pretty sure what I had to say was crucial to our mystery, but it vanished the moment I relaxed. Technically, everything I say is important, but this one had to do with the four-legged escapee…I think.

"Did you see Santa Claus pass by, Mrs. Barnes?" I asked, taking the time to finish putting on my jacket. I scanned town square, but there was no sign of St. Nicholas. "I was hoping to talk to him about Randy."

Cora regarded me with wariness, but that wasn't unusual. She thought my family was quite eccentric, with the exception of my mother. The two had decided to make amicable amends, but that was pretty much for the sake of appearances. Deep down the two women couldn't stand one another.

"Why on earth would the man hired to play Santa Claus know something about the missing reindeer? Really dear, you're just not thinking this through, are you?" Cora was carrying the kind of purse that had the short handles, but she made sure that the designer's gold logo was front and center hanging from its bright gold chain. I suddenly realized that she was dressed this way because she wanted to be caught on camera in the background of the mayor's interview. "Desmond and I are doing what we can to help with the search, of course. He's lucky he wasn't hurt earlier today when the other eight reindeer practically stampeded down River Bay. They could have killed someone."

There it is again. It's on the tip of my tongue, but I can't quite spit it out. Maybe I need to go back and eat another edible. The premium organic catnip that my BFF splurges on has health benefits, you know. It expands my mind and enhances my karma.

"Santa Claus was in town square when Randy went missing last night," I said, hoping that my excuse came across as plausible. "He was standing next to me, and he said something that came across as somewhat odd. I just wanted to have another word with him."

"Well, the mayor is getting ready to address his constituents. The interview was moved up to five o'clock from seven o'clock." Cora gestured toward the crowd, who all wanted a minute of fame on the local television. "He's invited me to speak on behalf of the combined search party effort, so I believe it would be best if I were there by his side when the interview commences."

Hey, do you think your mother's nemesis has the key to the city? It wouldn't surprise me if she was trying to melt it down for its gold value. She's power hungry, she's got her manicured fingernails into everyone's business, and she's the kind of person who would know the secrets of this town…such as where Skippy and his band of ninja squirrels hibernate during the winter.

I put on my cap that I'd dug out of my coat pocket as my gaze followed Cora to the intersection. Her head was held high and her regal stride was capturing attention of the local journalist and her cameraman, but I highly doubt she would know where the local squirrels hibernated in the winter.

That's it! See? I told you that my edibles have health benefits.

"What's it?" I asked distractedly, covering my lower face with my scarf before reaching into my other pocket for my gloves. The leather on my gloves was a lot lower quality than what

Cora's had been made out of, and now I was wondering if they contained any leather at all. Most of all, I was left marveling at St. Nicholas' ability to just vanish into a crowd unnoticed. "How does Santa Claus just disappear like that, Leo? I mean, he's wearing quite a lot of red, for crying out loud. I should still be able to catch sight of him in that crowd."

Are you not in the least bit curious as to what slipped my mind earlier?

Leo's memory blips happened so often that I'd gotten quite used to them. I turned to find that he was nowhere in sight, which was for the best. Since talking to Santa Claus was out of the question, I'd take advantage of Karen being at home if Leo's revelation didn't have us going in another direction altogether.

"I'm very curious, especially if it helps us locate the missing reindeer."

If the other eight antlered brutes heard the caribou whistle and busted out of their pen, wouldn't they do the same if they could hear their missing pal calling out?

"Leo, you're a genius," I whispered in excitement, reaching for the keys in my coat pocket. They weren't there. I must have left them in the back room of the tea shop. "It struck me as odd that Karen didn't pull into the garage. You know how Otis is about his car. What if she was the one to lure Randy away from his pen? The only logical place to put him until she could figure out how to return him after learning the truth about their circumstances would be the garage."

Seeing as you just called me a genius and we have to go back inside the tea shop, I believe that's grounds for another edible before we go breaking and entering into someone's garage. After all, one wrong added with another wrong makes a right, right? Or is that wrong? It's like adding negative numbers, or maybe I'm thinking of something entirely different. Either way, I get another edible.

Chapter Twelve

"I CAN'T SEE anything through the window," I whispered, cupping my gloves around my eyes to make it easier to see through the side door of Otis and Karen's garage. There was a thin vertical window near the doorknob, but it was too crusted with dust to see through the pane. "I don't hear anything, either. Leo, you're going to have to go inside and take a look around."

In case you've forgotten, the former sheriff and his wife own a dog. D. O. G. Dog. You know, a domestic cat's nemesis. FYI, those domesticated felines are so oblivious, they have no idea what is happening in their own backyards. Maybe I should hand out flyers.

"You can remain invisible," I prompted, not accepting the dog excuse. I stepped away from the door, having already debated knocking lightly to see if I could startle whatever was on the other side. I quickly discarded that idea. Who knew if Karen was inside the garage right this minute? How would I explain that I was sneaking around her yard? I wasn't the best liar. "Besides, Scooby is a Maltese. He's smaller than you are."

Another reason I shouldn't go inside. Who names a Maltese after a cartoon Great Dane? It's just not done, and now the poor whelp has a Napoleon complex. What do you think it's going to do to his mental state when he gets a whiff of me, but can't find me? He'll think he's losing what's left of his tiny mind. I know it might not seem like it, but I do have a heart, Raven.

This is when having Heidi by my side would have come in handy. She'd somehow learned the questionable art of picking locks in her youth. I found it best not to question some of her quirks.

"You're the one who said that Randy was most likely in a place where the other reindeer couldn't hear him calling out," I reminded Leo, stepping back to consider our options. I came up empty. Unfortunately, there really weren't any other alternatives other than to send Leo inside to make sure that Randy wasn't being kept prisoner by the former sheriff's wife. Good intentions aside, it wasn't fair to keep a beautiful animal contained inside four walls when his home was on acres and acres of open land where he was well taken care of and obviously loved by Barry Mina. "I thought you wanted the key to the town?"

That's bribery, Raven. You're playing with my emotions. Didn't we establish that we're not even sure that Paramour Bay has a golden key to the city?

"Is that a chance you're willing to take?" I asked, posing a question that I was confident Leo wouldn't be able to resist. And no, I experienced no guilt whatsoever. After all, we were talking about a symbol of Christmas, regardless that the man in the red suit indicated that Randy was actually a more famous reindeer in disguise. "Golden key equates to information on Skippy, and—"

Fine. I'm going inside, but don't blame me when the former sheriff and his wife have to take their zany furball to a pet psychologist. They exist, you know.

"Raven?"

I cringed at the sound of Karen's voice coming from around the front of the garage. I was busted, and now I was in the one situation where I had to think fast. Who would have thought witchcraft would have been easier to learn than the art of lying?

"Hi, Karen," I exclaimed after pasting a smile on my face. I dropped my arms to my sides, still attempting to come up with a plausible excuse as to why I would be sneaking around her property. My palm was as cool as a cucumber, and I was beginning to think my ability to sense danger had become defective. Why wasn't my gift working closer to town? "How are you doing?"

"I've had a busy day," Karen replied with a tilt of her head, wrapping her arms around the middle of her waist. She wasn't dressed for the cold, and she was clearly confused as to why I was standing next to the side entrance of her garage. It would help to know if Randy was actually inside the garage, but Leo hadn't made a reappearance. How hard could it be to spot a large reindeer in an empty garage? "Is there something I can help you with?"

I glanced down at the trampled snow, trying to find some way to answer her without outright accusing the former sheriff's wife of nabbing a reindeer from town square. Had Leo found something in the garage? Is that why it was taking him so long to reappear?

I'm here, I'm here. I got sidetracked by the delicious fragrance of fish. The former sheriff keeps his boat inside the garage, and I must say that it smells divine! As for the antlered brute, there was no sign of him or any tracks on the floor. Then again, the former sheriff does a splendid job of keeping that speckled paint void of any dirt.

"No, not at all," I answered in relief now that Leo had given me the perfect excuse. "The search groups are still out and about, and I thought I saw some hoofprints in the snow."

"Oh, we get a lot of deer around here." Karen motioned that I should follow her back to the front of the house. "Come on in out of the cold, dear. Can I make you a cup of tea?"

Say no. I'm not going inside with that mangy Maltese. Couldn't you hear him barking when he realized that a feline was in the garage?

Now that Leo mentioned it, the faintest sound of barking was coming from the house. This was my chance to find out why Karen had been acting so odd today, though. I wasn't about to pass up this opportunity.

"Everything okay?" Monty asked, standing in the driveway when we came around the corner of the garage. "Karen, what are you doing out here without your coat? You'll catch a cold like that."

"Oh, Scooby was barking and I just came outside to take a quick look as to what had him riled up," Karen said with a smile, though her cheeks were turning the same shade as Santa Claus' suit. She also held up some stale bread. "I needed to put some of this out for the birds, anyway. Found Raven following some tracks into the backyard. What are you doing home, Monty?"

Well, that explained what the stale bread had been for. I inwardly cringed at the way this situation was sliding and causing Leo and I to appear as if we'd overreacted.

How did I get on that overreaction bus? Contrary to the witch's guidebook, you and I are not attached at the hip, Raven.

"I closed up early," Monty said in frustration, giving a wave in my direction even though he was frowning in displeasure. "The mayor has everyone and their mother gathered in town square to watch that interview that they could all be viewing on their television sets. I have to drop this bucket off to the neighbor, and then I'm calling it an evening. I was out this morning to help with the search, but I don't want to overdo it with my back. Karen, were you able to get an appointment with the seamstress?"

Seamstress? Sweet angel of mercy, Raven! Do you realize what that means? That poor antlered brute was turned into some sort of rug! What kind of monsters are living in our quaint little town?

"Yes," Karen replied with excitement, even though she was already walking toward her front door. The wind wasn't so bad in the front of the house compared to the side, but she only had a sweater on for warmth. Leo sounded as if he were about to keel over upon hearing her reply. "I just got back home, as a matter of fact. Otis is going to be thrilled when he sees his Christmas present. Do you want the leftovers?"

Christmas angels are crying right now, Raven! This monster is trying to sell off the antlers as if they were nothing but spare parts. Oh, the horror of it all!

"If you don't mind me asking, what did you get Otis for Christmas?" I asked, ninety-nine percent sure that Karen wasn't talking about Randy. I shoved the guilt aside over the other one percent. It wasn't very nice of me to have that much doubt over the kindness of my neighbors, especially during such a holiday. "I'm still looking for ideas for my mother."

"I bought him slipcovers for the boat seats," Karen replied happily as she stood next to her front door tossing pieces of stale bread in front of her bushes. "The seamstress was able to hem the material after I measured the height. Plus, she's going to put in drawstrings on the bottom so that the fabric can close around the bottom post. I never would have thought of such a thing if Monty hadn't suggested it. It was worth all the running around today, especially since Otis has been out and about helping look for that poor reindeer."

Okay, so I might have overreacted just a smidge. In my defense, the antlered brute's fate was looking grim there for a while.

There was now no reason for me to go inside with Karen.

Her odd behavior hadn't been in relation to the abduction of Randy, and he certainly wasn't being held prisoner in her garage. I should be feeling relief, but I was now more anxious to find Randy than before.

Where could he be?

Did anyone think to check the farm? I'm not saying those ant-lered brutes have a high IQ, but even those mangy canines manage to find their way back home after getting lost. Why not a reindeer?

It was definitely an idea that I needed to throw out to Liam, who was currently with the mayor attempting to flush out the kidnapper…if there even was one. It was best I get back to town square. Besides, Mom and Heidi should be pulling into town soon.

"I'm glad it worked out for you," Monty said, holding up what appeared to be a bucket. It must be the item he needed to drop off at the neighbor's house. "You two have a good evening. I'm going to go drop this off now. You two enjoy your night."

"Come on inside, Raven," Karen urged me, twisting the knob on her front door. "I'll make us some tea."

"I really should be getting back to the search," I replied with a regretful smile. "Sorry about earlier. I didn't mean to scare you."

"Don't you worry about a thing," Karen exclaimed, stepping inside to get warmed up. "This is Paramour Bay. It's a good thing that the only thing we need to worry about is a reindeer wandering off, and I'm sure he'll be found in no time."

That's a pretty good outlook given that the coven war almost landed on top of the town's welcome mat not two months ago.

"Have a good night," I called out, quickly getting in my car and turning over the engine. Seeing as only around ten minutes had passed since Leo and I had gone to search Karen's garage, the heater kicked in well before I reached the main thoroughfare of town. "Leo, we're running out of ideas."

The pile of steaming brownies is still up for grabs...with me overseeing the project, of course. I do believe that the rubber gloves are still in the back seat.

Leo had materialized in the front seat, lifting his chin to enjoy the warmth of air coming from one of the vents. I could already see that my usual spot near the tea shop had been taken, most likely by someone already enjoying the festivities of town square or someone who wanted to witness the mayor's interview.

"The last resort at our disposal is the mayor's offer that there will be no questions asked if someone returns Randy to his pen tonight." I had no choice but to park near the bakery. Candy and Dee were walking out with what was probably hot chocolates in their hands, which they almost spilled thanks to little Bobby Hurst as he ran by. "I wonder if Bobby had any luck."

While I'm at my poker game tonight, I'll ask Ivan if he's gotten the privilege of escorting an antlered brute through the veil.

I winced at the thought of something horrible happening to Randy.

"Do you think something's wrong with my abilities?" I asked, truly wanting to know Leo's thoughts on the subject. "The palm of my right hand has only had a few tingles prickle my skin since Randy went missing, with the exception of Nan's special place in the woods. Usually in these types of cases, it would be so hot that I wouldn't even be able to wear my glove."

Which is even more reason to suspect that there was no foul play in the antlered brute's disappearance. Unless, of course...never mind. Forget I said anything.

"You can't say something like that and expect me to forget about it," I warned, prepared to bug him all night. "If you don't clarify what you were about to say, I will follow you to the poker game and wear mirrored sunglasses as I stand behind you."

That's low, Raven.

Leo and I then commenced in a staring contest in the front seats of my car, but I was prepared to do what was necessary if it meant finding out what could be causing my ability to be on the fritz.

I just want to go on record that you're going to freak out over nothing, because the chances of my random thought being the cause is less than that one percent chance of the former sheriff's wife being a reindeer serial killer.

"Fine," I relented, but only partially. "I'll take whatever you say with a grain of salt."

Technically, you should be taking what I'm about to tell you with a swig of eggnog, but whatever. There's a chance—and I personally don't believe it for a second—that otherworldly magic could be to blame for the energy fritz you seem to be experiencing.

"Otherworldly?" I asked, not following along. I do admit to being relieved that Leo didn't think whatever it was he was implying was possible. "You mean…"

Kris Kringle. Father Christmas. You know, good ol' St. Nicholas. But Santa Claus' existence has been an old wives' tale for many years, Raven. If it makes you feel any better, the chances of that being true are next to nil. It's about the same odds as the former sheriff's wife being a serial killer.

Chapter Thirteen

"MOM, IS THERE an old wives' tale about Santa Claus and our family lineage?" I asked, making sure I kept the question vague in case someone was walking past. We were standing by one of the portable heaters in town square, having met up with Mom and Heidi after they had to park near the Paramour Bay Inn. The festivities were now in full swing, and there wasn't a spot to be had along River Bay. "And have you noticed any...um, change in the air?"

Snap the head off a gingerbread man, why don't you? Hearing you tiptoe around the subject is torture. No one is around, not even the ho-ho-ho jolly red giant.

"If you're asking me if Father Christmas truly exists, then the answer is yes. Isn't the mere idea of St. Nicholas magic?" My mother was keeping a close eye on the mayor for some reason. She didn't seem to grasp what I was trying to ask. "You know the mayor better than I do, Raven. You don't believe he's culpable of staging this entire situation all to be the center of attention, do you? I mean, he did nab the headline on today's paper, and he's now been given his fifteen minutes of fame. I overheard that journalist mention that one of the national stations picked up the story as a feel-good piece."

The Mistress of the Dark certainly knows how to skim over the facts, doesn't she?

"I agree with your mother," Heidi said, popping the candy cane out of her mouth. "The mere idea of Santa Claus is magical. I used to try so hard to stay awake and listen for the sound of his sleigh landing on my roof on Christmas Eve. There was nothing better than running downstairs and finding all the presents underneath the tree, sans cookies and milk with the exception of a few crumbs left on the plate."

Speaking of crumbs, I bet I left some on my pillow back at the tea shop.

"I'm not talking about that kind of magic," I murmured, getting a bit hot standing so close to the heater. The volunteer firemen had also gotten the bonfire lit, so it was now a beautifully contained blaze with some of the kids already roasting marshmallows on long sticks. "I mean, real magic."

"You mean like a warlock?" Heidi asked, her blue eyes widening at the implication. "Noooo. You can't be serious. Wait. Can you?"

"Leo has been filling your head again with magical conspiracy theories, hasn't he?" my mother asked, stepping to the side when someone blocked her view of the mayor having a conversation with Cora and Desmond Barnes. When I grabbed the sleeve of her jacket so that she didn't get very far, she sighed in resignation. "St. Nicholas might be linked to our way of life. Is it true? I don't know, and I doubt we'll ever know. A missing reindeer and a heartfelt story about the herd doesn't mean a thing in the grand scheme of things. I mean, really, Raven. Of all the places in the world to visit, you think that Kris Kringle is going to be in Paramour Bay fourteen days before Christmas?"

Well, when Mom put it like that...

I told you that the chances were nearly nil, but you always get persnickety if I leave anything out. I know, I know. It's usually something more important than an old wives' tale, but you know that my memory issues don't distinguish between vital and random nonsense details. It's all because you've had me running around these past two days. How would you function on little to no caffeine? Don't think I didn't see that espresso you snuck out when we stopped by the tea shop.

"I think it's time I go say hello to the mayor, don't you?" my mother asked, patting the back of her hair where the top of her hat should have been. "And there's my dearest love. Beetle, over here!"

Ack! Hairball.

Leo wasn't actually hacking up a hairball. He was gagging at the way my mother doted over his best friend, which I agree tended to be a bit overboard. With that said, the two of them were very happy being with one another. My mother went off to grab Beetle by the arm and drag him over to where the mayor had just finished speaking with the Barnes. Considering how Cora and my mother felt about one another, it was a good thing that the Barnes had walked away before my mother engaged with the mayor.

"Here comes Liam," Heidi murmured, pointing toward him with her candy cane. "Maybe he has some news on the reindeer front. We seemed to have struck out with every lead, unless your mother's theory about the mayor is right."

"Heidi," Liam greeted with a nod, leaning down to kiss my cheek. "I spoke with Jack earlier. He got the word out to the state troopers patrolling the highways to be on the lookout for our reindeer. I'm hoping that the caribou didn't make it that far east. It's best for his safety that he stays close to this area, away from heavy traffic."

Tell me about it. I followed Skippy one day when he got an itch

*to hit one of the garbage cans on River Bay. I truly thought my
nemesis was going to be taken out by a green Jeep Wrangler. I'm all
for stopping the squirrelpocalypse, but I'm not too proud to admit
that I would have felt cheated at such a horrifying end.*

"Jack texted a bit ago and said that he'd try to drive out to
help with the search tonight."

"I made all the search parties call it a day. It's too dark outside, especially with this cloud coverage. The moon isn't even
visible to give natural light, and the last thing I need is for one of
the residents to get lost in the woods." Liam reached out and
touched my arm. "Hey, could I speak with you for a moment?"

*Can I sit this one out, please? Watching the Mistress of the Dark
fawn all over my BFF is about all I can take tonight.*

"Sure," I said, taking Liam's hand and following his lead. He
didn't stop until we'd passed the long line of parents and
children waiting for Santa Claus to make an appearance. The
man himself wasn't in attendance yet. After talking with my
mother, my belief that Kris Kringle could possibly be a warlock
of some sort sounded downright ludicrous. "What's wrong?"

Liam took the time to look around us, his need to do so
giving me that sinking sensation in the pit of my stomach. I fully
expected him to tell me that Randy had been found, but not in
the way we'd wanted to recover him.

"Does Barry know?" I whispered, tears immediately filling
my eyes as I thought of those poor eight reindeer in the pen who
were waiting for their friend to come back. I struggled to
maintain my composure. "Oh, Liam. This is just awful."

"No, no, no," Liam exclaimed, rubbing his hands up and
down my arms in reassurance. "Oh, sweetheart. I didn't mean to
scare you. We didn't find Randy. This is about the mayor's
assistant, Sheila."

The relief that rushed through my veins was vast, and it was like a weight had lifted off my chest. I used my glove to wipe away the few tears that had fallen, grateful that Liam was blocking everyone's view.

"Remember, I had Sheila checking into the individuals she hired for Paramour Bay's Winter Wonderland Festival. She found something that I need to follow up on," Liam said, lifting his gaze from mine to survey our surroundings. What or who was he looking for? "It turns out that no one was actually hired to take the position of Santa Claus."

Liam's interest in the holiday setting had me looking around, taking note of my mother talking up the mayor and Heidi somehow getting roped into roasting marshmallows. There was laughter and conversation floating in the air, but there was still a blanket of concern hanging over the festivities. Barry was standing inside the pen of the petting zoo looking forlorn as he rubbed the head of a caribou. I certainly wasn't expecting Liam to say something about St. Nicholas.

"What do you mean that she didn't hire someone as Santa Claus?" I asked, finally catching sight of the man in question. It was hard to miss the jolly *ho-ho-ho* as he made his way down the waiting line as he gave high-fives to the exuberant children. "I mean, clearly someone was hired."

"Sheila said the request somehow got lost when she gave the file to the employment agency. They never even conducted interviews," Liam revealed with a frown. "I need to talk to this guy. I'll be right back."

Before I could say another word, Liam began to weave his way through the numerous children who were waiting in line to sit on Santa's lap. As if invisible forces were against him from intercepting St. Nicholas from taking a seat in his big chair, one of the tiny elves carrying a ton of wrapped presents appeared out of nowhere. I could only gasp in horror as the two of them ran into one another, causing all the gifts to go flying into the air as Liam did his best to steady the woman before she landed in a heap on the ground.

Did I miss an episode of "Andy Griffith"? The good ol' sheriff never really reminded me of Barney Fife, but I can always adjust my vertical hold.

Leo was visible as he came sauntering out from behind one of the blow-up penguins that had been positioned off to the side. He plopped down next to my winter boots, most likely enjoying the show of Liam scrambling to pick up the various sized boxes. In all the commotion, Santa Claus had actually made it to his chair and was waving that white glove of his with a twinkle in his blue eyes.

"No one hired a Santa Claus to be here," I murmured, figuring everyone was too busy rushing to help Liam and the elf to overhear me. "Liam was attempting to go and talk to him when…well, that happened."

I gestured toward the commotion, but me being in the middle would have only made it worse. My accident-prone tendencies had a way of doing that at the most inopportune times.

Again, the chances of ol' Kris Kringle over there sitting on his throne being the real deal is as low as the former sheriff's wife being a reindeer serial killer. In the meantime, you'll be happy to know that I found Elsie's reading glasses. Once I show you where and you collect them, I'll have done my good deed for next year. See that? I'm ahead of the game. Maybe. For some reason, I think I was supposed to mention something else to you. Whatever it is, it escapes me.

Before I could ask where Leo had spotted those elusive reading glasses, I saw my mother coming toward me with Beetle in tow. From the determination written across her features, it was evident that she'd found out something worth sharing.

"Mom, what is it?" I asked, checking on Liam. He'd been able to gather the presents with the help of the elf and some of the parents standing in line. "Were you right about the mayor?"

"The mayor?" my mother asked, giving me an exasperated look like she hadn't had the brilliant idea that the mayor could have staged all this hullabaloo. "I don't know, Raven. I didn't get a chance to find out anything with all the excitement going on with you. What on earth happened to Liam and that elf?"

"I'm honestly not sure," I replied, seeing Liam sidestep a little boy who was running up the red carpet that led to Santa Claus' lap. He was still waving, though I wasn't so sure it was to the children as much as it was to Liam. "Liam wanted to have a chat with St. Nicholas about the fact that no one was hired to dress for the part. It's a long story, but the paperwork got lost in the shuffle. Now we have no idea who this guy is or where he came from."

"What does that have to do with the elf?" Beetle asked, though he really only knew part of the story. My mother just smiled and patted his hand in reassurance. "If that Santa Claus had something to do with the missing reindeer, then Liam should bring him in for questioning. Yes, siree, he should."

My mother was shaking her head to my nonverbal question about the possibility of Kris Kringle being more than a regular jolly man dressed in a red suit. She still refused to believe that the possibility of magic might exist in this situation, which was quite ironic considering that we were witches.

I'm sure this is not going to help our situation, but I'd like to point out that maybe the percentage of Karen being a reindeer serial killer just shot up to two percent.

Chapter Fourteen

"OH, YOUR SHERIFF is really going to do it, isn't he?" my mother murmured as we all watched Liam follow close behind the small boy who had already made his way to Santa Claus. "I do give him credit for following through on his oath to protect and defend."

Liam knelt as he put his hand on the little boy's shoulder, gesturing back toward the line and to where his mother was waiting with a concerned frown on her face. My mother was right about Liam's need to protect this town, even if it meant disappointing the boisterous children waiting their turn to tell Santa Claus what they wanted underneath the tree come Christmas morning.

Don't worry about the residents labeling the good ol' sheriff as that green monster without a heart. Once they realize that the former sheriff's wife is a reindeer serial killer, the focus will be on her.

"I'll be right back," I muttered to my mother and Beetle, gesturing for Heidi to join me as I made my way around the throngs of people now wondering why Liam wanted a private moment with Santa Claus. It didn't take long for Heidi to shove the burnt marshmallow into her mouth and fall into step beside me, though she was still licking her fingers. "Liam found out that no one was hired to fill Santa Claus' spot, if you know what

I mean."

Seeing as we were walking past the end of the line where parents were attempting to figure out what was going on and the children were becoming antsy, I was very careful with my words. Heidi understood exactly what I meant, though.

"Don't we want to find out if you know who is the genuine article?" Heidi asked, her blue gaze practically glued to the big chair that was now the center of attention. "Let me just say that it would be really nice to know why I didn't get that Easy-Bake oven I wanted when I was eight years old."

Um, does Heidi know that she can't cook? I was there the day she decided to make that oaf of a detective dinner. I had no idea that it was possible to burn boiling water. Should the jolly one turn out to be Father Christmas himself, I'm sure his gift that year was making sure the Connolly residence didn't burn to the ground.

"I want to ask Barry Mina a question that goes along with that line of thought." It didn't take us long to reach the petting zoo, but I came to an abrupt halt when I saw the mayor and Barry Mina off to the side having a heated argument. "You don't think Mom was right about the mayor's involvement, do you?"

"Excuse me." A high-pitched voice came from our left. Heidi and I both turned to find the elf that Liam had run into with a present in her hand. "Are you Raven Lattice Marigold?"

Those pointy ears should be illegal. And aren't elves supposed to have bells on their stockings so that the jolly man can hear them coming from a mile away?

Heidi nudged me in the arm when I didn't answer right away. In my defense, I was trying to figure out how a strange elf could know my full name.

The way I figure it, there are two ways that went down. Either this mini-Spock overheard your mother talking to Beetle about how exasperating her only daughter was or the odds of the former sheriff's wife being a reindeer serial killer just shot up another percent. What are we at now? Three? When we get to five percent, I'm writing that letter to Santa Claus about the catnip farm I want in Alaska.

"Yes, I'm Raven," I replied, looking down at the wrapped present the elf held up for me to take.

"This is for you," the elf replied with a smile and a tilt of her head.

Leo had been plopped down on his haunches in between me and Heidi, but he jumped back when one of those pointed ears aimed in his direction. I didn't blame him. Those things appeared quite sharp.

"For me?" I reiterated, sounding like a simpleton. This elf had specifically sought me out, so of course the present was for me. Only I had no idea who she was or why she was giving me a gift. "Who is this from?"

Really? An elf who works for Kris Kringle gives you a wrapped present with a glittery bow, and that's the question you ask?

"Santa Claus, of course," the elf replied with a high-pitched giggle. "He wanted me to tell you that the sheriff should use his annual budget for other things, but that you'd appreciate the gift more for your future endeavors. I better get back before all the little boys and girls get too anxious. Merry Christmas!"

The present that the elf had basically plopped into my arms was quite heavy. I wasn't about to open it in the middle of town square, but there really wasn't anywhere I could go without getting curious stares and losing my opportunity to insert myself into the conversation that Barry Mina was having with the mayor.

Too late. Hey, since we're over this way, we should—

"Mayor," Heidi called out, causing me to hoist the present

for a firmer grip as I turned to find that the mayor's wife was practically dragging him away from the petting zoo by the arm. Heidi's quick thinking stopped the couple in their tracks right in front of us. "I just had to say that your offer for whoever might have taken the reindeer last night to return him with no questions asked was genius. You never cease to amaze me about how deeply you care for our community."

"Oh, thank you, Miss Connolly," the mayor said with a beaming smile. I noticed that his wife seemed to relax a bit now that they'd walked away from Barry Mina, whose squinted gaze was practically shooting daggers at the mayor's back. "Thank you very much. We can only hope that if the reindeer didn't wander off on his own, that whoever took him will take this opportunity that we are affording him or her. I'm all for protecting our wildlife, but that poor thing wouldn't last long out there in the wilderness all by himself."

Why that no-good—

I hadn't realized that Leo had been working himself up into a tizzy over the mayor's ease at which he was taking credit for an idea that wasn't his, all to look good in the eyes of the residents. The way Leo had leaned down on his two front paws with his wiggling butt high in the air told me that he was mere seconds away from sinking his claws into the mayor's pant leg.

I'm not sure how I didn't drop the large present in my arms, but I managed to exchange the present for Leo in one swift motion. How my back muscles didn't seize was beyond me, but I was able to set my familiar on top of the glittery bow without missing a beat.

"Oh, look at that handsome tomcat," the mayor's wife cooed, leaning down and running her leathered glove over Leo's head. She began using the tips of the leather to scratch behind his ears, which had him purring louder than the kids shouting in excitement about something behind me. The mayor's wife glanced up from her affectionate duty. "It looks as if Liam is done talking with Santa Claus. Look at all the children. I just love this time of year."

And I love this woman, Raven. Yeah, right there. A little more to the left. Ahhhh…perfect.

I stood up straight so that I could stretch my back and see for myself that Liam had allowed St. Nicholas to continue his job duties. Sure enough, Liam was shaking Santa Claus' hand, white glove and all. Did this mean that Sheila had been wrong about the agency hired to employ the staff for this year's festival?

"Mr. Mina still seems pretty upset," Heidi continued, not one to be drawn off her target. She was like a dog with his bone…or Leo with his premium organic catnip edibles. "Is there anything we can do?"

"No, no," the mayor responded with as much vigor. "Mr. Mina is obviously concerned about the wellbeing of his missing reindeer. He was just expressing his displeasure at the sheriff's decision to suspend the search after dark. I did my best to reassure him that we would start back up at daybreak."

My attention was torn between Liam walking toward us and the mayor basically throwing him under the bus. The majority of the searchers were the older residents, doing their part to help someone who brought a petting zoo to town in order to entertain the children. Liam had made the right decision to suspend the search, all the while making certain that other law enforcement officers patrolling the highway were on high alert. The mayor was attempting to take all the credit while deflecting all the blame. It wasn't fair.

Don't go getting your dander up, Raven. This is the best head scratch I've had in days. Give me a few seconds of peace, would ya?

"Mayor," Liam greeted, resting his hand on my lower back as if to let me know that he could handle himself. I'm sure he could, but that didn't mean a spell to have the mayor flub up the next time he went on national television hadn't crossed my mind. "I checked into that matter that Sheila brought up, and you'll be pleased to know that all the paperwork is in order. There was a mix-up at the agency, and Mr. Nickels got a frantic call from someone there asking if he'd fill in at the last minute. He was well aware of the situation, and he was able to give me more information than Sheila. I'll follow up with her tomorrow morning about getting things squared away."

"Excellent news," the mayor replied with a beaming smile, though his relief had more to do with the fact that a criminal wasn't posing as Santa Claus. "All we need to do now is find the missing reindeer, return him to his rightful owner, and then spread the good word via another interview."

Leo's sigh of regret could be heard when the mayor's wife dropped her fingers from the back of his neck so that she could return to her husband's side. She wrapped her arm through his and then patted his hand as if to chastise him.

"I know that it's important to you to let the public know the missing reindeer is safe and sound, but we must remember that this is the season of giving," the mayor's wife reminded him gently. "Whoever finds this precious Randy should be reward-ed."

Did you hear that, Raven? The mayor's wife said the R word, and I'm not talking about Randy. She said reward, as in R-E-W-A-R-D. You know what the equates to, right? You guessed it. The golden key. Not only does this lovely woman know how to scratch behind the ears, she's selfless when it comes to recognition. I might have to hit the campaign trail. She clearly deserves to be mayor over that attention-seeking boor.

"Of course, of course," the mayor agreed with a vigorous nod. "Unless, of course, someone anonymously returns the large animal. It would fall on my shoulders to alert the media, of course. These types of situations are followed closely by those outlets to spread the feel-good happy endings, you know."

The fact that the mayor would say such a thing had me believing that maybe my mother was onto something. First things first—who had given me a wrapped present? Now that Liam had rested my concern over St. Nicholas, it was highly doubtful that this gift had been from the jolly man himself.

"Oh, there's Gillian Murphy," the mayor's wife exclaimed, lifting a gloved hand in order to wave to someone behind me. "Liam, Raven. If you'll excuse us, we must go say hello to an old friend."

A slightly bitter cold breeze broke through the strategically placed heaters as if in warning, though the palm of my hand hadn't varied in temperature since...well, the beginning of this case, actually.

Defective or the former sheriff's wife is actually—

"Did you have that elf give me a present?" I asked Liam, cutting off Leo. Karen Finley wasn't some reindeer serial killer, which meant that Santa Claus was simply a man wanting to do his part this holiday season. "She sought me out and said that she had a gift for me from Santa Claus."

If Liam had asked the elf to bring me a present, it was a sweet gesture. My smile continued to grow the more I thought about such effort being put into my gift, ignoring the fact that there were still fourteen days before the big event. I wasn't much on surprises, anyway.

This better be an appropriate gift to give someone in public.

Leo hopped down, albeit ungracefully, leaving the red bow

flattened against the wrapping paper. He then sat back on his haunches, having a front row seat to the unveiling.

"I wish I could say that was from me, but yours is safely tucked under the Christmas tree at home," Liam said, frowning as he glanced down at the present. "You said the same elf who I ran into earlier gave you the present?"

"Yes, and she did so with a message about it being able to save your annual budget." In retrospect, I realized what it could be and quickly knelt down to unwrap the gift. "Liam, I think—"

"Don't open it," Liam warned, but he was a smidge too late. I'd already ripped the side of the paper without thought to the ribbon still secure around the box. "Is that an actual drone?"

Liam quickly knelt by my side and joined me in untying the ribbon and took the rest of the wrapping off. Sure enough, we were looking at a drone set with all the trimmings.

Hey, Raven. I know my short-term memory has been iffy these last two days without getting my steady supply of tasty edibles, but didn't that elf say that the jolly red giant gave you that present?

I quickly glanced over my shoulder to find that Santa Claus was indeed staring directly at us. The streetlamp above him must have caught his glasses just right, because there was no way that I should be able see the twinkle that practically sparkled like a diamond in his eye from our location.

I would definitely call that a twinkle, Raven. There's only one way good ol' Kris could have known about your conversation regarding the drone, which has me changing my mind about everything. I mean, this is a revelation. That twinkle is proof...and right before our very own eyes! I'm now a full believer, and I need to write out my wish list for Christmas morning. Oh, this means you might want to go and have another conversation with the former sheriff's wife. She's definitely a reindeer serial killer, and she needs to be stopped.

Chapter Fifteen

"I SPOKE WITH Mr. Nickels," Liam insisted, handing me a steaming cup of coffee that he'd poured from a thermos. "It's one thing to believe in the supernatural, but Santa Claus? I'm telling you, he was a nice gentleman who didn't hesitate to show me his driver's license. There doesn't seem to be anything unusual about him."

Am I the only one who thinks we look like idiots camping out in the petting zoo and attempting to blend in with the antlered brutes? Not to mention this place smells worse than my litter box, and I like myself. I shouldn't have skipped tonight's poker game. Remind me again how I allowed you to talk me into this charade?

"Does the name not strike you as odd?" I asked wryly, gratefully taking the hot beverage. The bale of hay we were sitting on was actually quite warm, and the wooden structure meant for the reindeer did provide adequate protection from the wind. Leo was on top of a small straw bed that Barry must have spread out for the caribou. "And I'm pretty sure we said that the guilty party could bring Randy back with no consequences, so we're technically going against the accord."

"That's not what we're doing here, Raven. Besides, Mr. Nickels comes across as one of those men who gives insight to his wisdom." Liam carefully turned in the small wooden edifice, careful not to spill his own coffee. "Scoot."

I managed to inch over to make enough room for him, but apparently not as gracefully as Liam. A bit of coffee sloshed over the rim of the plastic cup and onto my glove.

Liam and I had taken the drone and stored it inside the tea shop for safekeeping. We couldn't use it at night, so we'd have to wait until morning to break it out in order to have an aerial view of the town. Meanwhile, the batteries were charging the required eight hours before first use.

With a little prodding, Liam had sought out Mr. Nickels to get clarification on the gift, but all the man said was that this time of year was magical and we should be thankful for what gifts we receive. I could see where Liam would consider advice such as that wisdom. After all, there was a lot of truth behind his adages. As for the elf, she'd apparently gone home early because she was nowhere to be found.

Shhhh. I'm already thinking about my wish list. It's the only thing that's keeping me sane now that Ted might actually win the pot tonight. Do you think the Alaska catnip farm is better than the one in Honduras? It's hard to make a decision when I haven't tasted either of those delicious edibles in over three hours.

Basically, the rest of the evening had been uneventful. Upon Mom and Beetle calling it a night, Heidi had done the same with the promise to rejoin the search come morning, if needed. We were all still hoping that someone would take the mayor up on his public offer to bring Randy back to his pen without any consequences. It was when I'd gone to say goodnight to Liam that I'd discovered his intention of staking out the pen tonight.

"First off, the man's full name is Steven Nickels." Liam held up a hand when I rolled my eyes at the similarities in the initials. One of the streetlamps afforded us enough illumination to see one another. "I have his home address. To be sure and to alleviate your concern, I've already sent the information to Jack. I asked him to run Mr. Nickels through the database to make sure that he is who he says he is. In the meantime, I'm not sitting on this pile of hay in hopes of making an arrest. We made a promise to the public, and I stand by our word."

Wait just a frozen snowflake! What am I doing asking for a catnip farm when I could actually ask for a winning battle plan against the squirrelpocalypse? I'm a genius! This might actually be worth missing tonight's poker game.

"Staking out the pen to see who returns Randy doesn't actually feel as we're standing by our word," I pointed out, taking a sip of my coffee to find that it had the perfect mixture of cream and sugar. I closed my eyes in enjoyment, not having a lot of moments like this one today. There were times I drank my coffee black, but that was when necessity came into play. "It seems more like a trap."

Yes, yes. A battle plan with a trap. Keep going, Raven. You're on a roll.

"We're not here to arrest anyone, Raven." Liam transferred his coffee to his left hand so that he could put his right arm around me for some additional warmth. "I promised Barry Mina that I would keep a close eye on the other eight reindeer. They still refuse to leave the pen."

"So, what will you do if someone returns Randy?" I asked, feeling a lot better now that I had some coffee in my system. I could see one of the reindeer walking toward us through the opening. "Just pretend that we're not here?"

"Exactly," Liam replied, settling back against the wall to get comfortable. It was like he'd done this before. Then again, he'd been employed by the NYPD earlier in his career. He'd probably been on a few stakeouts in his time. "Besides, no one can see us in here. The reindeer's excitement over the return of Randy will provide us cover."

Uh, what is that antlered brute doing hanging around the entrance of our temporary abode? Does he not know we have this space reserved for the night? The good ol' sheriff should have run this stakeout by those eight giant creatures who live here. They can squish me without blinking an eye, you know.

Sure enough, and almost as if to verify that Liam was telling the truth, one of the reindeer began to make his way into the wooden structure. They were magnificent creatures, with their large antlers and their brawny bodies. There was also almost a sadness in those dark brown eyes, and it was all I could do not to throw my arms around his neck and tell him that his best friend would be okay.

I wouldn't do that if I were you. We've already established that if Santa Claus is real then the former sheriff's wife might have done something unspeakable. Let's face it. Who better to have the Serial Killer Handbook than someone who is married to a former police officer? It's genius, really.

"What are you and Leo talking about?" Liam asked, his words more of a soothing murmur as he settled in for the night. He was definitely in his element. "I can always tell when the two of you are conversing. His longest whisker twitches."

It's a good thing that the good ol' sheriff isn't part of our supernatural poker game. He wouldn't have a dime to his name. Come to think of it, maybe I can talk Ivan into letting that actually happen. I could make a mint.

"Leo's whisker actually twitches when he's annoyed." I paused for a second, realizing what I'd said. It was kind of funny now that I thought about it. "I guess I do annoy him most of the time, but right now he's worried that you didn't run this entire stakeout thing past the reindeer. One of them looks set to join us."

"Leo, these reindeer are the gentlest of animals,' Liam said reassuringly, lifting the plastic cup of coffee to his lips. He finished speaking before taking a drink. "I promise that they won't hurt you."

"Leo also thinks that Karen Finley is a reindeer serial killer."

Liam immediately inhaled the coffee upon hearing such a ludicrous statement, sending him into a coughing fit. He leaned forward and pressed the back of his glove to his mouth as he tried to recover.

Ludicrous statement? Wasn't it you who was convinced that the former sheriff's wife was involved in the reindeer-napping caper?

"In Leo's defense, I did believe that Karen might have been involved in Randy's disappearance," I confessed, not able to throw Leo under the bus like that. Liam was finally able to draw in some oxygen, but he was still unable to talk. That was probably a good thing until I explained myself a bit more. "You see, it all started when we were at Wilma's house checking to see if she'd noticed anything unusual in her yard. She has a ton of those bird feeders outside of her kitchen window. I was hoping that Randy had walked through her yard or something. Anyway, as Leo and I joined Mom on the sidewalk, Karen was pulling into her driveway…and she didn't even bother to wave."

Had we been talking about anyone else, I'm pretty sure neither one of us would have thought anything of the small slight. With that said, Liam understood very well that it wasn't in Karen's nature not to acknowledge somebody.

"I'll admit that doesn't sound like Karen, but I'm confused as to how you and Leo could go from a distracted individual to an all-out serial killer," Liam said once he'd semi-recovered. He attempted to clear his throat once more before continuing. "I'm sure that Karen didn't see you standing across the street. Besides, she was pretty busy today running around getting Otis' Christmas gift."

"That's the thing," I admitted, knowing that Liam wasn't going to like what we'd done. "She did see us, but she was just in a hurry. Unfortunately, I didn't know that she was preoccupied. When I was at the diner, Paula mentioned that Karen had been into the diner to see if they had any stale bread. We made an assumption and thought maybe she'd gotten it for Randy. On top of that, Karen didn't acknowledge me again when I was standing in front of Mrs. Salisbury's residence. I hopped in my car to follow Karen, but I lost her."

"You lost her?" Liam asked, skepticism lacing his tone. "How can you lose sight of someone on the side streets of Paramour Bay?"

"Exactly," I said, glad that Liam was starting to see things my way.

I wouldn't say the good ol' sheriff is coming round to our way of thinking, Raven. I do believe he is wondering how we make it through a day without tripping over our own feet and paws. Hearing you tell the story also has me marveling at our survival instincts. This doesn't bode well for the squirrelpocalypse.

"I thought it was suspicious enough to warrant further investigating, so Leo and I decided to go take a peek inside Otis and Karen's garage." I held up my hand when Liam's jaw fell open an inch. Saying all this aloud did have me rethinking some of our decisions, but Leo and I had determined that is was always those we least expected in times like this. "It's not like we actually thought she did something horrible to Randy, but more like she was attempting to help him. Remember when Otis and I talked in your office about the fact that a lot of people didn't realize the story behind the reindeer? Well, I thought maybe Karen had believed she was helping them. Does that make sense?"

I don't think you should have ended that explanation with a question, Raven. You should...um, we definitely have a nightly visitor. Shoo. Go away now. Skedaddle, antlered brute.

"Just look at him, Liam," I whispered, holding out my hand to our curious visitor. I was ecstatic when the reindeer inched closer, his nostrils flaring as if to sniff out any danger. He must have decided that we were okay, because the caribou leaned his nose down for me to pet. "They're magical in their own right, and I can see where somebody didn't understand their history or how they came to be with Barry."

Don't squish me. Don't squish me. Don't squish me.

Leo had his eyes squeezed closed as he repeated that little prayer in his head, as if this gentle reindeer would do anything of the sort.

"I can understand why you would have thought Karen would want to help, but all you had to do was ask me about Karen. I would have told you that she was trying her best to get her errands done before Otis got home. He tends to always know what she gets him, but she has a plan in place this year."

Speaking of plan, do we have one to get this antlered brute to leave before he decides to lay right down on top of me? I'm all for losing a pound or two, but not in the form of a flattened pancake.

We all startled when the reindeer snorted and suddenly turned around, heading back outside to the pen. Leo might have eked out a squeak of terror when one of the reindeer's hooves came awfully close to his head, but I couldn't be sure over the sounds of the eight reindeer.

Stampede!

There was no stampede, but the reindeer had become anx-ious over something. The question was had someone decided to take the mayor up on his public offer or was Liam going to have to make an arrest before another reindeer-napping occurred right in the middle of town square.

I was just giving you fair warning. It wasn't like I was panick-ing or anything. Tell me again why I had to cancel my poker game tonight?

"Looks like we finally have a visitor," Liam whispered, using his right hand to grab ahold of my arm. He'd already set down his coffee in anticipation of what was to come. "We remain silent in here in case someone is returning Randy. If there are signs that somebody is here to try and take another reindeer, I'll go out and take care of the situation."

I nodded my understanding, though I wasn't too worried that someone was here to do harm to us or these animals. The palm of my right hand wasn't warm in the least. With that said, I still tensed in anticipation as Liam leaned forward on the bale of hay in expectation that someone was heading in our direction to have another go at a reindeer-napping.

Haven't we already agreed that you're having a slight malfunc-tion in that area? It's due to the genuine article in the red suit whom I must befriend now that there's a way to get that Alaskan catnip farm come Christmas morning. I'm a believer, Raven, which means this reindeer-napping has to be stopped at all costs!

Chapter Sixteen

"YOU LOOK LIKE—"

"Not another word," I warned Heidi, who had just entered the tea shop. As a matter of fact, the echo from the bell above the glass door was still resonating in my ears. I took another sip of my much-needed coffee. "I got home around two-thirty in the morning, and I didn't get to sleep until three. I need a bit more caffeine before we head out."

Neither scenario that Liam or I had predicted had come true last night. No one had shown up to return Randy, but neither had anyone stopped by the petting zoo to take one of the other reindeer. The person who had raised such a commotion with the caribou had been none other than Barry Mina. He hadn't been able to sleep, too worried about Randy and the others.

"Barry showed up at the petting zoo last night," I divulged, carefully taking a seat on the stool behind the counter. I'd opened up the tea shop a little earlier than usual, so I didn't expect Beetle to show up for another ten minutes. I honestly wasn't sure what I would do without him. "You should have seen him with those reindeer, Heidi. He adores them and vice versa. He is definitely off the suspect list."

Heidi had tiptoed over to Leo, who was currently sacked out on his pillow in the display window. All four paws were sticking up in the air, and his tongue was hanging from the side of his mouth as a slight snore occurred with every breath.

"Poker?" Heidi asked softly, making her way over to the coffee station. I'd just finished brewing all the tea samples, as well as creating the perfect carafe of Columbian coffee. "Ivan and the rest of the group are going to have to start monitoring his edible intake."

"Not poker," I replied with a smile. "I talked Leo into helping me and Liam keep watch over the reindeer last night. He wasn't too happy, but he now fully believes in Santa Claus. He's been busy making his wish list."

"Are you really going to buy him a catnip farm in Alaska?" Heidi had taken off her gloves so that she could make herself a cup of coffee. I'd already put one of my travel mugs out that I'd brought from home, knowing that she'd want to take it with her when we headed out this morning. "I can't believe you even researched them."

"Believe it or not, I reached out to an owner who said he would actually be willing to draw up a contract that states Leo owns one percent of the farm," I whispered, having already cast an itsy-bitsy spell to ensure that Leo couldn't read my thoughts on this particular subject. "I made a deal with the pet shop here in town. Thelma, the owner, agreed to sell the catnip brand from this particular farm in exchange for free tea leaves."

"Why would that convince the catnip owner to give up one percent of the farm?" Heidi had opted for red earmuffs this morning, but she'd slid them down around her neck so that she could hear me clearly. She'd already added the second scoop of sugar to her cup and was in the process of grabbing one of the wooden stir sticks from the box. "I don't want to know, do I?"

"Trust me, all the finagling worked out. Leo's name will actually be on the paperwork, though that took quite a bit of coaxing on my part." I rested my elbows on the counter, inhaling the delicious aroma steaming out of my cup. I'd yet to put the lid on, knowing full well that I'd pour myself another refill before heading out into the cold. "Anyway, Barry Mina is definitely off the suspect list."

"You said you cleared Karen Finley. That leaves St. Nicholas, though didn't Liam rule him out as being the genuine article?" Heidi asked, walking around the counter. She motioned with her hand that she wanted a bit of room on my stool. I scooted over a bit so that she could share the cushion. "I have to say that I also find it hard to believe that Santa Claus truly exists."

"I haven't had time to conduct the proper research, but I did manage to look some sites up on my phone when I was getting dressed this morning." I'd been keeping a close eye on the police station across the street, waiting for Liam to park his truck by the curb. He said last night that he'd flown a drone before, so it made sense for him to be the one to operate the gift I'd been given last night. "I kept coming back to the same truth with every site—magic exists in every form. Basically, Mom was right. Santa Claus does exist, which can only mean that the existence of Krampus is authentic, by the way. That's for another time, though. We have enough on our plate already."

Heidi had turned her head to look at me, her lips parted to ask more about this Krampus figure, but she choose wisely. She even shook her head a bit, as if to remind herself not to bite off more than she could chew. Thankfully, she chose to stay on topic.

"So, you're saying that we have the real deal in Paramour Bay." Heidi paused as if she needed to digest that information. "I might be in trouble, Raven. I've never had a lump of coal in my stocking."

I laughed, and it struck me in this moment how lucky I was to have those I loved around me again. Heidi moving here and setting up her own business had only fortified our friendship even more, and my mother…well, it was good to have her close by, even if she did have her own motives for doing such a thing. I leaned over a bit so that my shoulder bumped into Heidi light enough that neither one of us spilled our coffees.

"You've got a heart of gold, woman," I stated matter-of-factly so that she couldn't argue. "I know that, the town knows that, and now Santa Claus knows that. As a matter of fact, good ol' St. Nick has gotten to see for himself that this community has come together to help a defenseless animal in need."

"Witches, werewolves, grim reapers, and now Santa Claus." Heidi shook her head, her blue eyes wide with astonishment. "Never in my wildest imagination did I think we could possibly live a life such as this."

"Don't get me wrong," I warned, knowing that we had quite a lot to do on the agenda today. "I'm still not one hundred percent convinced that we have the authentic Santa Claus in town. I mean, there are things that just don't add up. Take for instance the reindeer's names or the fact that Steve Nickels had an actual license with a physical address that is nowhere near the North Pole."

"You do realize that we live in a society where skeptics run amuck by the millions, right?" Heidi asked wryly, pointing out the obvious. She took a sip of her coffee now that it had cooled down somewhat. "I'll admit to being guilty of being one of those cynics once in a while, but I kind of like the idea that Kris Kringle actually exists to bring joy to the world."

"Heidi, no one has ever accused you of being a cynic in your entire life," I said with a laugh. Eventually, my chuckles faded as

I thought over our current situation. "I just realized how sad it is that our only suspect in a reindeer-napping case is Santa Claus himself."

"Really? Father Christmas is our only suspect?" Heidi sighed, practically sliding off the stool in dejection. "We're pitiful. I'm beginning to think Leo's idea to collect piles of steaming brownies might not be such a bad idea."

"It's a little late for that, considering Barry Mina cleans out that pen almost every hour on the hour." I couldn't help but feel sorry for the man. I know how despondent I would be if something ever happened to Leo. "Thinking over our lack of leads, I'm beginning to think that maybe Randy did wander off on his own. We made the assumption that Bobby Hurst was the only child who snuck the reindeer their sugar cookies."

"It still doesn't explain the lack of hoofprints," Heidi pointed out, setting her coffee down on the counter as she readjusted her earmuffs so that they covered her ears. "I mean, it's like Randy walked right out of town square and trotted down River Bay without anyone the wiser."

"It's possible," I said, thinking back to that night. "Think about it. Almost everyone had either been in line to visit Santa Claus, was part of the epic snowball battle, or roasting marsh-mallows around the bonfire. That doesn't even include the townsfolk listening to the carolers. Who is to say that Randy just didn't open the latch with his nose and then head out in search of more sugar cookies?"

The bell above the door rang as Beetle made his grand entrance. As usual, he had a big smile on his face. I did my best not to connect that grin with my mother, because it wasn't right for a daughter to think of a parent in that manner. Instead, I just assumed that he was happy to see me and Leo.

Speaking of Leo, I caught the slight signs of him stirring coming from his cat pillow. He had the ability to catch the scent of catnip from miles away, even in his sleep.

"Good morning, ladies and gentleman," Beetle exclaimed, his white flyaway hairs still bent back with his momentum. "Good morning. I predict that today is the day that Randy the Reindeer will make his way back home, the winter wonderland can proceed with the delightful holiday spirit, and the town can concentrate on the essence of giving from their hearts."

Heidi and I both shared smiles as Beetle's infectious attitude lifted our spirits. As for Leo, he'd shaken off the remnants of sleep and was waiting eagerly for his special treat.

I love this man, Raven. Oh, how I love him so.

"Good morning, Beetle." I jumped down from the stool a bit more ungracefully than Heidi had a minute earlier, reaching for my jacket that I had laid over the cash register. "I was able to get some various tea samples brewed, along with a carafe full of hazelnut coffee. The tourists seem to love the flavored blends this time of year."

"Perfect," Beetle said, having already greeted Leo with one of those catnip edibles in the shape of a Christmas tree. His gift included a pat on the head, which Leo soaked up like a lapdog. "Just perfect. You two go out there and bring home that reindeer. Don't worry about a thing. Not one thing. I have things covered here."

I might have to stay inside today and keep my BFF company, Raven. We wouldn't want him to get lonely, would we?

Seeing as Beetle was walking my way with the intention of storing his coat in the back room, I bit my tongue before automatically replying to Leo's question. In all the commotion last night, I never did retrieve Elsie's reading glasses. I wanted to take care of that errand while Liam got the drone working this morning.

Don't go ruining my special treat time, Raven. I'll just tell you where the reading glasses are so that you can collect them. The red-rimmed reading glasses are near the drainage cover next to the curb by the hair salon. You go retrieve them, I'll go back to sleep, and you can then come back when the good ol' sheriff is ready to fly the drone. I'd like to see how he uses it so that I might try that type of intelligence gathering on Skippy come spring.

"Call or text me if you have any problems today," I said after I'd zipped up my jacket and began to work on my outer accessories. "I'm running this drone over to Liam before paying a visit to Elsie. Did Mom mention that she was meeting us over at the station?"

"My sweetheart was enjoying a breakfast of pancakes that I made her before leaving the house this morning." Beetle had come back through the string of ivory-colored fairy beads, letting them fall behind him in a melodic melody. His green and red bowtie complimented his green cardigan sweater perfectly. "However, she does have every intention of helping the towns-folk search for Randy. I'm sure she'll heading into town straightaway."

"Beetle, did I tell you about my meeting with Cora and Desmond?" Heidi asked, diving into the details while I finished tying my scarf around my neck and collecting the drone case. Heidi had already grabbed my travel mug, putting the lid on it so that the contents wouldn't spill. "I'll keep you posted on how things go from here, but I'm really pleased with how things are going. You did a fantastic job keeping records. I appreciate the care you put in making the transition easier for me."

"I'm glad to hear it, dear. Very glad," Beetle replied with

vigor, taking his place behind the counter when Heidi and I both began to make our way to the front door. "Be safe out there!"

"Leo," I murmured out of the side of my mouth, noticing that he was feigning another nap. "Let's go."

Heidi cradled one of the travel mugs in her arm, opening the door for me as I managed to carry the hard case outside. The cold blast of air was kind of refreshing, but that only lasted a few seconds. A quick look down the block revealed that town square was quiet this time of the morning, and would likely remain so until early this afternoon when the festivities began. I did take a moment to inhale deeply, loving the pleasant scent of burning wood that always seemed to be in the air this time of year.

"Leo found Elsie's reading glasses somewhere alongside the curb near the salon," I said as we walked toward the intersection. "Once I drop this off with Liam, I'm going to go collect them and drive them over to her. Do you want to come with me?"

"Sure." Heidi gestured toward the box. "Why don't I take the box over to Liam, you and Leo collect the reading glasses, and then we'll meet by your car? I parked down near my office, because I do need to work this afternoon."

It took us a few seconds, but we were able to exchange items without dropping anything. Heidi now had the drone case in her possession while I had the two travel mugs in my hands. Leo had finally appeared, though it was clear that he wasn't happy from the way he was sauntering ahead on the sidewalk.

"I won't be long," I told Heidi, quickly catching up to Leo. "Hey, the reason I wanted to get you out of the tea shop was so that I could ask you an important question."

You're seeking my advice? Carry on.

I smiled when Leo slowed his pace, always liking when I

turned to him instead of my mother. He hadn't been too happy with her move back to her childhood home. In his opinion, he already had to share me with Ted. Throw in my mother, and it was like a free for all in the magical realm of the Marigolds.

"Say that Santa Claus actually turns out to be the genuine article," I tossed out speculatively, concentrating on the palm of my right hand. The travel mug was slightly warm, which was the only reason I had any heat in my skin. "That still doesn't explain why his presence would cause my ability to go on the fritz."

If we are dealing with the authentic Father Christmas from the 1700s, then that kind of magic is more powerful than we've ever encountered. You realize that he can deliver presents to close to twenty million houses in under sixty minutes? That's time distortion.

"So why wouldn't I feel more energy rising up from the earth then?" I asked, still not grasping the effects such a presence would have on magic. Then again, I hadn't been the best student in high school when it came to physics. "You'd think my hand would be as hot as a baking sheet right out from the oven."

What energy? All the energy in this area would be attracted to one thing—Father Christmas himself.

"Wait a second." We'd finally made it to the hair salon, though Candy didn't seem to have any early appointments just yet. The shop was still dark inside. "Are you saying that casting spells with Father Christmas around the vicinity would be useless? Has he drained the batteries?"

Leo didn't answer right away, which led me to believe that I'd asked him a question in which he wasn't sure of how to answer. I'm glad I wasn't the only one who had trouble understanding physics.

Seeing as I've never been in the presence of what some would consider royalty among the supernatural, I suggest we have your

mother try casting a spell and see what happens. You know, in case it
backfires or fizzles and she turns into an elf or something.

"I'm not having Mom do anything of the sort." I stepped off
the curb and began to look for a set of red-rimmed reading
glasses, hoping they hadn't been run over by a car. We were close
enough to town square that parking was off limits, but that
didn't mean everyone obeyed the signs. "She's been relatively
nice since she moved back to town last month. Even you have to
admit that she's been on her best behavior. Leo, where did you
see Elsie's glasses? I don't see them, so maybe someone else
picked them up."

By the drainage thingamabob. See? The reddish rims blend in
with the rust color of the metal.

"Found them," I exclaimed with delight, bending at the knee
to retrieve the glasses. I used my glove to wipe off the snow and
mud. "Can you believe that there isn't a scratch on them? Elsie is
going to be so—"

I stopped talking when something else colorful caught my
eye.

Uh-oh.

"Uh-oh?" I quickly took off my glove so that I could fit my
hand down inside one of the slats of the drainage cover. "Leo,
this is a bag full of baby carrots."

I knew there was something else I was forgetting to tell you last
night. Raven, I also discovered a bag of carrots yesterday. I'm sure
there's a reasonable explanation as to why there is a bag of carrots
caught on the metal of a drainage cover.

"That explanation would be what we first suspected—that
someone lured Randy out of the pen," I surmised, not liking
where my thoughts were taking me. I lifted the red-rimmed
reading glasses in proof. "Oh, Leo. This isn't good. I think I

know exactly who took Randy."

Look at you, Raven, solving crimes without the use of magic. I should mark down my mentoring in the good column for Father Christmas. Witchcraft or not, we've turned out to be excellent in the amateur sleuth business. I do believe this offsets those actions against Skippy and his band of ninja squirrels that might be considered naughty, if you catch my drift.

Chapter Seventeen

"RAVEN, I STILL don't believe that Randy could have been marched down River Bay away from town square without anyone seeing a thing," Heidi exclaimed, standing right next to me as we stood in front of Elsie's house. Sure enough, Wilma's vehicle sat smackdab in the middle of the driveway. "And by an elderly woman at that."

"It makes sense. Think about it," I urged Heidi, confident in my sleuthing skills. Technically, Leo was the one who had solved this caper. "Wilma bought Elsie those pink-rimmed reading glasses she'd been wanting, but she was still in a funk over the red ones. Then Elsie called Wilma before she could head over, only for me to see her in the pet shop."

Upon discovering the bag of carrots dangling from the drainage cover, Leo and I had quickly made our way down to the pet shop. Thelma quite happily talked about the fact that Wilma had bought one of those oversized dog beds, even needing help to stuff the large item into the trunk of her car.

Now we know why the antlered brute didn't try to break out of prison. Those old biddies are treating him like a king. Remember, I tried sleeping on that bed of hay, and it certainly wasn't a picnic. I bet they're serving him sugar cookies by hand while he lays on that plush material as if he found paradise.

"Wilma bought an oversized dog bed with the excuse that

she was going to put it outside for the bunny rabbits." I sighed, not exactly sure how I was going to handle the situation. Heidi had met me at my car, and we drove straight here without telling anyone my theory. This was something that needed to be confirmed first, and I was thankful that my mother hadn't shown up at the station before we had driven into one of the side neighborhoods. "And don't forget that I saw Wilma drive past Mrs. Salisbury's house, heading straight here as if she were on a mission...most likely with the oversized dog bed in the trunk of her car. I'm telling you, Randy is either in Elsie's house or the garage."

"Well, how do you want to play this?"

You're going to make me go into that garage, aren't you?

"Yep," I replied, not worried that Heidi would misinterpret my answer. I did clue her in on the conversation, though. "I'm sending Leo into the garage to check on things first. If he finds Randy, then we'll ring the doorbell and wing it. I have no doubt that Elsie was doing what she thought was right, and Wilma would do anything to protect her best friend."

"I get that," Heidi replied, tossing a smile my way. "Okay, Leo. Strut your stuff, you handsome tomcat."

My beloved Heidi does have a way with words, doesn't she?

Heidi and I both leaned back against my car, not worried about getting our snow pants dirty. The material was easy to wash. Plus, we had no idea how long we would have to wait. Leo was known to get distracted by the simplest things. I guess we could have waited inside the car, keeping the heat on and staying warm. With that said, this snowsuit I'd splurged on last season was quite toasty.

"Did I tell you that your mom wants to start coming over once a week to teach me some spells?" Heidi asked to pass the time, no hesitation in her tone whatsoever. "We did talk about me becoming a hedgling or something like that, and I would feel better if I knew something to help with this war that's brewing between the factions"

"A hedge witch," I corrected her with a snort, having already agreed that Heidi needed to learn the basics just in case the coven war spilled over into Paramour Bay. Even though the palm of my hand seemed defective recently, I could still sense the warmth coming from the black tourmaline stone embraced in silver filigree. Nan had sent me a message from beyond the grave that this stone played an important role in the upcoming conflict. "Heidi, I think the brewing is all but done. Rye has been out of town for days, and that could only mean that the war has escalated between the factions."

"Let's just say that I sensed a lot of tension up in Windsor, and that was just by driving through your Nan's old neighborhood." Heidi adjusted her earmuffs after a gust of cold wind had woven its way in between the houses. "Leo is certainly taking his time. Have you decided what you're going to do if Rudy is inside that garage?"

"Randy," I corrected her, taking the time to look over Elsie's yard. The driveway had been shoveled and salted, and the blanket of snow appeared untouched. "Maybe I am wrong. I mean, just because Elsie's reading glasses were near the drainage area where the open bag of carrots had fallen in between the slats doesn't mean a thing. Coincidences do happen."

"Well, it's not like a reindeer would fit into Elsie's compact vehicle. I'm not sure I could fit in that small contraption she calls a car," Heidi shared, keeping her watchful gaze on the garage door. "Which means that Elsie would have had to walk from town to here. I'm one hundred percent positive that she didn't do that, Raven."

"I agree, but—"

I'm giving you my notice now, Raven—I'm leaving. I'm packing my bags and moving in with the old biddy. I've already accepted that I'll have to invest in those reindeer ear thingamajigs. It's clear that the reindeer abductor prefers antlered brutes over handsome tomcats, but that's easily remedied.

"I knew it," I whispered in victory, still having no idea how in the world Elsie could have gotten Randy here all by herself. Not to mention that Wilma wouldn't have been a big help in that department, either. "Heidi, Randy is inside that garage. Follow my lead."

I didn't waste time, knowing that the search parties were gathering at the police station right this minute. Liam was also getting the drone ready to fly over the remote parts of town. It was time to bring Randy home for the holidays.

Seriously? I say I'm moving out, and all you're worried about is getting that antlered brute back into his pen? I'm recommending that good ol' St. Nick put you on his naughty list.

Heidi fell into step beside me as we made our way up the small path, no doubt Leo somewhere close by. There was no chance that he would miss out on how this situation was about to go down. We stepped up onto the porch where Elsie had hung a pine wreath with a red bow on her front door. Neither one of us expected it to swing open, causing one of the cones to fall off and land at our feet.

Oh, this ought to be good. Don't be too hard on my new land-lords, Raven.

"Hello, darlings," Wilma exclaimed with a nervous smile. She was all bundled up in her burgundy winter coat, scarf, and hat. She clutched her matching gloves in one hand, all but forcing us to take a step backward as she slammed the front door closed behind her. "Elsie is feeling a bit under the weather. I wouldn't bother her right now. I was just heading to your shop to grab her some tea. Why don't you follow me back into town and help me pick out a blend that can help with a cold?"

As much as I adored these two women, I couldn't let them continue to harbor a reindeer that wasn't theirs to keep…no matter how good their intentions might have been.

"Wilma, we know."

"You know that Elsie isn't feeling good?" Wilma said, feigning surprise. "Well, aren't you two sweethearts for dropping by to see if she's okay. Don't you worry about a thing. I'll let her know you stopped by."

And here I thought you were a bad liar. I guess I can look on the bright side—I'll always know when she's hiding my edibles.

Wilma was pretty fast on her feet, and she had all but made a beeline back inside the house. It was all due to Heidi that the front door wasn't slammed in our face.

"Raven means that we know that the missing reindeer is here," Heidi declared, somehow knocking the wreath off its hook and right into my face. The only thing that saved my face from a bunch of pine needles was the large velvet red bow. "Please let us come inside, and we'll talk about your options."

Options? There is only one option here, and that is to take the antlered brute back to his herd so that I can take his place. Did you know that not only did these old biddies buy him the most expensive dog bed—I should know, because I just looked at the price tag that is still attached to the bed—but they bought him one of those plush holiday blankets with reindeer printed on the material. I bet they have one of those blankets with cats.

Wilma muttered something about how she knew this was

going to happen as she finally let us inside the warm living room. The design was just how you'd imagine a single elderly woman's home to be, with floral print couches, lace doilies, and houseplants galore…only most of the ferns had been knocked over onto the carpet and there were dirty hoofprints tracking every which way but out the front door. Oh, and there wasn't the smell of homemade chocolate chip cookies in the air. Instead, the foul odor of what could only be referred to as a combination of wet dog and those piles of steaming brownies Leo mentioned the other day hung heavy in the air. As if that wasn't enough evidence of Randy's presence, a frantic cockatiel was chirping up a storm with a string of what could only be interpreted as complaints.

"Wow," Heidi murmured in disbelief underneath her breath as she closed the door behind us. We could only stand inside the entryway in shock, doing our best not to inhale the rancid smell too deeply. "Just…wow."

I take it back. I have an aversion to dirt and odors. You can thank me now for not marking the house in any way shape or form.

"It's not as bad as it looks," Wilma exclaimed, doing her best to reassure us even though her thin lips were quivering. She was still clutching her gloves, only she'd pressed them tightly against her nose. "Elsie! Elsie, get in here right this minute!"

"…coming. Don't get your panties in a twist, Wilma." Elsie had entered the kitchen through a small hallway that clearly led into the garage. "I haven't figured out how to get that precious reindeer back to his—"

Elsie had made it all the way through the kitchen before she realized that Wilma wasn't the only one in the living room. She came to an abrupt halt, her slippers gripping the tiled floor as if they'd become stuck in glue.

Too bad I didn't bring one of my edibles with me. This is highly entertaining.

"Wilma, you should have told me we had guests," Elsie said with a tumultuous smile, as if her living room didn't look like a dirt bomb had exploded over the beige carpet. She then faked a cough hard enough to send her into a real fit. She held up her hand when Wilma expressed her concern. "I'm fine, I'm fine. As you can see, I'm under the weather."

Heidi and I both looked down at the mud tracks that crossed lanes like multiple train tracks before settling our attention back on Elsie, letting her know that we weren't fooled. It was best that she tell us the truth.

"I've let the housework get away from me, haven't I?" Elsie shook her head as if she were chastising herself. "I'll have to get straight to that once I'm feeling better."

This old biddy is one tough cookie. She's not going to crack, Raven.

Leo was absolutely right. The only way I saw Elsie confessing to harboring a reindeer was if Randy himself waltzed into the kitchen.

Would you look at that? It's as if you said the magic words, Raven…no pun intended.

Sure enough, the clonking of hooves against the soiled tile echoed throughout the kitchen. Elsie and Wilma were staring at one another in horror. To their credit, Wilma recovered first and carried on the charade as if they were actresses in a Broadway play.

"Elsie, you must have left your garage door wide open," Wilma exclaimed in feigned disbelief, edging a few inches away from the path that Randy seemed to want to take—which was straight for Heidi and me. "Isn't that the reindeer that went missing from the petting zoo? What a coincidence."

"Isn't it?" Elsie asked, agreeing with a rather animated nod. "Someone must have realized what a terrible mistake she—"

"Or he," Wilma corrected, shooting Elsie a warning glance so that she would choose her words more carefully.

"You're right, Wilma. Someone must have realized what a terrible mistake she or *he* made upon luring this precious animal away from his friends. I'm sure that she or *he* thought they were doing the right thing in wanting to return them to the wild, but recognized too late that the reindeer were right where they belonged upon hearing the mayor speak last night," Elsie said, still nodding vigorously as she did her best to finagle out of this predicament she'd found herself in. "Raven and Heidi, do you think you could lead him back to his home? I'm sure the other reindeer are missing their friend terribly."

Elsie and Wilma were both looking at Heidi and I expectantly, leaving us to make the final decision. Did we call them out on what a terrible choice had been made, or did we allow them to wrong a right?

I'm going to go with the latter, since I'm trying to make the nice list. You know, just in case the man in the red suit is the genuine article. My wish list includes that Alaskan catnip farm, blueprints for the squirrelpocalypse, one of those fuzzy blankets, a scratching...

"We'll take Randy back to the petting zoo where his owner and herd are very worried about him," I said, stressing the fact that Barry and the other caribou were deeply concerned about their friend. Heidi had already gotten a handful of oatmeal out of her pocket and was holding out her hand to keep Randy from destroying anything else in the house. "I can understand how someone might have had good intentions only to realize they didn't have the full story."

"Exactly," Elsie and Wilma said in unison. Their relief was almost palpable. I guess one could say the penance of causing such worry and chaos with the townsfolk and Barry Mina was being left with a house that would take days to get back into order. Elsie wasn't one to waste time, either. "I'm suddenly feeling a lot better. Wilma, why don't you take your coat off and stay awhile? We can watch one of the morning talk shows while you help me tidy up a bit."

Heidi nudged me with her elbow, indicating that we'd best leave well enough alone. There was still the question of how an elderly woman with such a small car had transported Randy from town and deep into one of the neighborhoods without anyone the wiser.

Oh, I can answer that. These old biddies are not to be messed with, Raven. They're wise beyond their years. You see, there is a carrot tied to the bumper of that contraption in the garage. The antlered brute must have followed the car slowly down the middle of River Bay, which would explain why there were no tracks or piles of steaming brownies in the snow.

I'd stepped back so that Heidi could open the front door and lead Randy outside. He seemed happy to do so, even lifting his front hooves as if he were ready to prance and dance his way back to his herd. It was as if he'd taken a two-day vacation, soaked up the luxuries he'd been provided by the staff, and was ready to head home.

"Oh, here are your reading glasses," I announced, holding out Elsie's spectacles. Wilma was closest, so she was the one to step forward and take them. "You must have dropped them in the no-parking zone next to town square."

"Silly me," Elsie said with a nervous laugh, not quite confident that I was willing to let this situation slide. This was the season of giving, though. "I must not have put them in my purse for safekeeping. I'll be sure to make better choices, Raven."

Speaking of choices, do you think that having six items on my wish list it too much to ask for from Father Christmas?

Elsie's vague gesture of regret was enough for me to know that Elsie would think twice before acting spontaneously ever again. She'd reacted drastically without having all the facts, just as I had in the past on several occasions. Numerous, actually. Weren't we all guilty of that in our daily lives? The end result was that she was now trying her best to figure out a way fix her mistake.

Heidi and I would help Elsie give Randy the happy ending he deserved, and the holiday festivities could continue on without missing a Christmas beat. The season of giving was upon us, and letting bygones be bygones fell into that category.

Bygones? Does that mean I have to get your mother a present?

"I have something special for you ladies at the tea shop, so you'll have to come in before Christmas to get your gifts," I said teasingly, watching the tension ease out of both women as if they were steam coming off two cups of hot tea. "Enjoy your morning!"

I had no doubt that both women had collapsed on the couch in exhaustion the moment I closed the front door. Maybe I should have asked for that carrot that was still attached to Elsie's bumper. Watching Heidi play with Randy in the snow had me wondering how we were supposed to get him back into town. It wasn't like he could fit in my car, either.

"Looks like we're walking back to town, Heidi." I came down the porch steps as I took off my glove, holding my hand out when I got close to him. Randy immediately came forward and let me rub the side of his face. "Hey, fellow. I don't know if you lead Santa Claus' team of reindeer, but we better get you back with the others just in case. What do you say?"

I made the decision to stick with six items. Six is a good even number, right? Chop-chop, Raven. Let's get this antlered brute back with the others so that they can get ready to do their job come Christmas Eve night. As I've said from the very beginning...ho-ho-ho!

Chapter Eighteen

"WHERE'S LEO?" MADDIE asked with a frown, looking everywhere for my familiar. She'd appeared so suddenly that I'd almost dropped one of the hot chocolates that the football team had been selling at their table to raise money for new uniforms. "I have something for him."

"Leo should be here shortly," I told Maddie with a reassuring smile. "He was finishing up dinner when I left the tea shop. I'll be over near the petting zoo if you'd like to check back with me in a little bit."

"Okay."

And just like that, Maddie ran off to join her friends in the snowman building contest. The winter wonderland was in full swing once again, everyone celebrating the return of Randy the Reindeer. Technically, the festivities had kicked off earlier this afternoon, but it was now going on six o'clock in the evening. Santa Claus was due any minute, and the children who had yet to tell him what they wanted for Christmas were eager to have their turn on his lap.

As for Barry Mina and the rest of the herd, they hadn't left Randy's side since this morning. Barry had even mentioned that it might be time to load up the caribou and take them back to their sanctuary, but the reindeer all refused to leave their pen. It was clear they wanted to stay, and Barry was too soft-hearted to make them do anything they didn't want to do after being separated for two days.

There were only a few people who knew the truth about Randy's little adventure, and that was Liam, my mother, and Beetle. Heidi and I had explained to them what had taken place, along with the fact that Elsie had been trying to figure out a way to get Randy back to town without anyone being the wiser. Mom had pointed out that with Wilma's help, Elsie could have coaxed Randy back into town the same way she'd lured him out, but Beetle reminded her that people Elsie and Wilma's age needed their beauty sleep.

At the end of the day, it didn't matter. Paramour Bay was back to normal, and the winter wonderland festivities were in full swing. I spotted Liam talking to the mayor near the petting zoo, both having already given another interview this afternoon regarding Randy's return. The Christmas carolers were currently singing about a snowman running through town, and I was grateful that we didn't have that mystery to solve. It was bad enough that Jack had contacted Liam regarding Steve Nickels. He was an upstanding man who had been legitimately hired by the agency to play the part of Santa Claus. I'd accepted that my abilities hadn't been waylaid by Father Christmas absconding with all the surrounding energy, but instead that there hadn't been any ill will meant toward Randy at any point.

I'm pretty sure that Leo had torn up his wish list, especially since he'd changed his tune once again. He'd muttered *bah humbug* after each bite of his dinner. Nothing I said about having a bit of faith seemed to put a dent in his bad mood. I'd left him to sulk, deciding to join the others for a bit of fun.

"For you," I announced, handing Liam one of the hot chocolates. He replied with a kiss and settled his hand on my lower back. Now that I wasn't intending to go traipsing around town, I'd traded my snowsuit in for one of my broomstick skirts, my favorite pair of knee-high black boots, and a red turtleneck to match the festive mood. I'd topped it off with a warm leather jacket and matching gloves that had once belonged to my Nan. Her taste in clothes had been impeccable. "Hello, mayor."

"Good evening, Miss Marigold," he exclaimed with a slight bow. "I want to thank you personally for your help in returning Randy the Reindeer. I already spoke with Miss Connolly earlier, but she was wrangled by my wife to help at the gift wrapping table. It's good citizens like you who are the heart of Paramour Bay."

Bah humbug.

"I'm glad that Heidi and I were in the right place at the right time," I replied with a smile, glad that Leo had decided to join us after all. He wasn't the only one. "Oh, look. There's my mother and Beetle."

"Perfect. I've been meaning to speak with Regina," the mayor said, surprising both me and Liam. Beetle had stopped to speak with Cora Barnes, much to my mother's dismay. She wouldn't be the one to leave first, though, and she would stand there with a pasted smile on her face until the conversation had ended naturally. "She inquired about an heirloom in my family that has been handed down for generations. I didn't even know it existed, yet your mother thought my sister might have a pendant dating back from the 1800s."

I didn't think it was possible, but my evening just got worse.

"A pendant?" Liam asked, already knowing from the way my jaw was mimicking a fish that I couldn't find my voice. "Does it hold some meaning to Regina or—"

The mayor was already walking toward my mother, not

hearing Liam's questions. I grabbed ahold of Liam's jacket sleeve with my left hand in dismay. He was rubbing my back in support, but the only thing that would give me reassurance that my mother wasn't involving herself in coven business was hearing that directly from her.

Your mother is getting a lump of coal in her stocking. And to think I was in a giving mood earlier. Bah humbug!

"You rescued Randy the Reindeer today, Raven." Liam gazed down at me with absolutely no doubt in his dark eyes. There was something to be said for somebody having complete faith in you. "You can handle anything thrown your way. I'll go insert myself into the conversation and send your mother over this way. Talk to her. I'm sure that whatever she's trying to do is for your protection."

Your mother's name went back on the naughty list, Raven.

Leo had been invisible, but his anxiety that my mother might be dabbling in the coven war had him making a physical, yet disheveled, appearance from around an inflatable penguin. His longest whisker was twitching uncontrollably.

"Ho-ho-ho!"

All four of Leo's feet came off the ground. All I can say was that I was grateful that the football team had put disposable lids on the cups of hot chocolate. Steve Nickels was dressed in his red suit, black belt, and gold-rimmed glasses. His blue eyes twinkled with merriment.

"Hi, Santa Claus," I greeted, keeping most of my attention on my mother. Liam was, indeed, trying to insert himself into the conversation and all but pushing my mother my way. "Did you hear that Randy was returned to Barry Mina?"

"Yes, I did. What wonderful news," Santa replied, patting the black buttons on his red coat in relief. I did manage to spare a glance at his long white beard, wondering how he got it to look so real. "Christmas Eve will now go off without a hitch, thanks to you, my dear."

Here we go again with the irritating pretense of being Father Christmas. Well, speaking of giving, we don't have time for this exchange, Raven.

"I'm glad we could help," I said, going along with Mr. Nickels in case one of the young children overheard us.

"Well, who else would I want on the case but the best amateur sleuths in the business?" Santa Claus whispered as if we'd just conspired to abscond with all the presents from the elves. "Ho-ho-ho!"

Uh, Raven? How would this man in the red suit know about our nicknames if he…Christmas on a cracker! It's Kris Kringle! It's St. Nicholas! It's Father Christmas himself! Quick…what are my six things? I need to write them down again!

"Wait," I called out, almost surprised when Santa Claus actually stopped and turned around. There was that infectious twinkle in his blue eyes again. "Are you…"

I realized that it was foolish of me to ask Santa Claus if he was real in front of eagerly waiting boys and girls. As if he understood my predicament, he winked and called out another ho-ho-ho.

"You already know the answer, my dear Raven." Santa Claus had leaned down and used his hand to prevent others from hearing him. "My Rosemary said you were a special one. She was right. Thank you—and Leo, of course—for saving Christmas this year."

Santa Claus lowered his hand and belted out one of those jolly laughs, leaving me and Leo quite speechless with such an announcement.

"Merry Christmas!"

Leo and I were left behind to watch in disbelief as Santa Claus began to make his way to his chair. Santa Claus was real. The original St. Nicholas had actually graced Paramour Bay with his magical presence. And the most surprising thing of all was that Father Christmas had known my grandmother.

"Leo?"

What can I say? Short-term memory loss. It does make life exciting, doesn't it? I mean, discovering that Santa Claus is real for the second time is even better than the first time around! I think. You know what this means, right? We're on the nice list!

I couldn't help but laugh out loud in happiness at the knowledge that we'd met Father Christmas himself. It was an honor, and he'd even thanked us for making sure that he could deliver presents to all the boys and girls around the world. Liam, my mother, Beetle, and the others turned to see what had happened, so I wiggled my fingers and enjoyed my hot chocolate. I would share the news with them later, and I would even postpone grilling my mother about whatever pendant she was trying to acquire from the mayor.

"Hey," Heidi said somewhat breathlessly, appearing out of nowhere. "What did I miss?"

Only the best thing ever—Santa Claus! 'Tis the season to believe, and as the famous poem states...Merry Christmas to all and to all a good night!

~ THE END ~

It's a baffling time when quirky dreams become reality in the next mystifying installment of the Paramour Bay Mysteries by USA Today Bestselling Author Kennedy Layne...

kennedylayne.com/baffling-blend.html

It's that time of year when winter's icy grasp is still hanging over the area, yet a few hopeful hints of spring are dangling in the crisp air. You know that moment when the feeling of regret has everyone on edge and thinking that maybe they should have gone ahead and taken their vacation in the deep south where the sun is still shining and warm, the birds are merrily chirping, and dreams are just dreams.

That's not the case in the quaint coastal Connecticut town of Paramour Bay. Raven Marigold is flummoxed when not one, not two, but three shockingly realistic dreams have come true in the span of only one week. She might be a witch, but she knows for certain that she isn't psychic. When a fourth dream reveals a wicked witch casting a fatal spell upon one of the Marigolds, it's a race against time to prevent her nightmare from coming true.

Bring your comfy pillow and a magical dreamcatcher if you want to help Raven and the gang attempt to solve this latest mystery pertaining to vision of winter's most frightening forecast!

BOOKS BY KENNEDY LAYNE

HEX ON ME MYSTERIES
If the Curse Fits
Cursing up the Wrong Tree
The Squeaky Ghost Gets the Curse
The Curse that Bites
Curse Me Under the Mistletoe

PARAMOUR BAY MYSTERIES
Magical Blend
Bewitching Blend
Enchanting Blend
Haunting Blend
Charming Blend
Spellbinding Blend
Cryptic Blend
Broomstick Blend
Spirited Blend
Yuletide Blend
Baffling Blend

OFFICE ROULETTE SERIES
Means (Office Roulette, Book One)
Motive (Office Roulette, Book Two)
Opportunity (Office Roulette, Book Three)

KEYS TO LOVE SERIES
Unlocking Fear (Keys to Love, Book One)
Unlocking Secrets (Keys to Love, Book Two)
Unlocking Lies (Keys to Love, Book Three)
Unlocking Shadows (Keys to Love, Book Four)
Unlocking Darkness (Keys to Love, Book Five)

SURVIVING ASHES SERIES
Essential Beginnings (Surviving Ashes, Book One)
Hidden Ashes (Surviving Ashes, Book Two)
Buried Flames (Surviving Ashes, Book Three)
Endless Flames (Surviving Ashes, Book Four)
Rising Flames (Surviving Ashes, Book Five)

CSA CASE FILES SERIES
Captured Innocence (CSA Case Files 1)
Sinful Resurrection (CSA Case Files 2)
Renewed Faith (CSA Case Files 3)
Campaign of Desire (CSA Case Files 4)
Internal Temptation (CSA Case Files 5)
Radiant Surrender (CSA Case Files 6)
Redeem My Heart (CSA Case Files 7)
A Mission of Love (CSA Case Files 8)

RED STARR SERIES
Starr's Awakening(Red Starr, Book One)
Hearths of Fire (Red Starr, Book Two)
Targets Entangled (Red Starr, Book Three)
Igniting Passion (Red Starr, Book Four)
Untold Devotion (Red Starr, Book Five)
Fulfilling Promises (Red Starr, Book Six)
Fated Identity (Red Starr, Book Seven)
Red's Salvation (Red Starr, Book Eight)

THE SAFEGUARD SERIES
Brutal Obsession (The Safeguard Series, Book One)
Faithful Addiction (The Safeguard Series, Book Two)
Distant Illusions (The Safeguard Series, Book Three)
Casual Impressions (The Safeguard Series, Book Four)
Honest Intentions (The Safeguard Series, Book Five)
Deadly Premonitions (The Safeguard Series, Book Six)

ABOUT THE AUTHOR

First and foremost, I love life. I love that I'm a wife, mother, daughter, sister… and a writer.

I am one of the lucky women in this world who gets to do what makes them happy. As long as I have a cup of coffee (maybe two or three) and my laptop, the stories evolve themselves and I try to do them justice. I draw my inspiration from a retired Marine Master Sergeant that swept me off of my feet and has drawn me into a world that fulfills all of my deepest and darkest desires. Erotic romance, military men, intrigue, with a little bit of kinky chili pepper (his recipe), fill my head and there is nothing more satisfying than making the hero and heroine fulfill their destinies.

Thank you for having joined me on their journeys…

Email: kennedylayneauthor@gmail.com

Facebook: facebook.com/kennedy.layne.94

Twitter: twitter.com/KennedyL_Author

Website: www.kennedylayne.com

Newsletter:
www.kennedylayne.com/meet-kennedy.html

Made in the USA
Columbia, SC
26 January 2020